THE PRISONER OF
Pineapple Place

ANNE LINDBERGH can hardly remember *not* writing. Born in New York City, she grew up in Connecticut in a house filled with books. Since her parents—Anne Morrow Lindbergh and Charles A. Lindbergh—were both writers, she was encouraged in her own writing of poems and stories, which she began at an early age.

Anne Lindbergh lived in Paris off and on for fifteen years and now lives in St. Johnsbury, Vermont. She is the author of several popular books for young readers, including *The Hunky-Dory Dairy, Nobody's Orphan, The Shadow on the Dial, The Worry Week*, and *The People in Pineapple Place*, all Avon Camelot books.

THE PRISONER OF
Pineapple Place

ANNE LINDBERGH

AN AVON CAMELOT BOOK

AVON BOOKS
A division of
The Hearst Corporation
105 Madison Avenue
New York, New York 10016

First Avon Camelot Printing: August 1990

CAMELOT TRADEMARK REG. U.S. PAT. OFF. AND IN OTHER COUNTRIES, MARCA
REGISTRADA, HECHO EN U.S.A.

Printed in the U.S.A.

OPM 10 9 8 7 6 5 4 3 2 1

For Charles once more, with love

THE PRISONER OF
Pineapple Place

Mrs. Pettylittle sighed and put the lid back on the garbage can.

Nothing. No magazines or newspapers, not a scrap of cloth, not even an empty jar.

At least the can was clean: there wasn't the slightest grease spot on her neat, black gloves. For once she wouldn't have to wash them after work, but that was hardly a consolation. She had been out since dawn, and her shopping bags were empty. What was the world coming to?

There was a nip in the air. She pulled her fur tippet snugly around her throat before moving on to the next trash container. She would try for half an hour more, and then go home.

Sitting in the patrol car down the street, Officer Rossotti sighed, too. "Beats me!" he said over the radio to headquarters. "It's the first time I ever seen a bag lady in this town. She's dressed wrong, too. Fur piece, hat, gloves—the works. Not your run-of-the-mill vagrant."

The radio spat out a scratchy answer.

"I'll keep an eye on her," Officer Rossotti promised. "But what I'd like to know is, where the heck did she come from?"

The First Day

1

On the morning after his street moved to Athens, Jeremiah Jenkins climbed to his secret place in the cedar tree, near Mr. Sweeny's house. It was a place the other children didn't know about, where they couldn't find him. From there, if he was lucky, he might hear Mr. Sweeny talking to his wife through an open window. And he would see over the rooftops of Pineapple Place to the outside world.

The outside world. What would the view be today? For fifty years on mornings like this—the first morning after a move—Jeremiah had climbed the cedar tree for a first glimpse of his new neighborhood. Pineapple Place had moved so often that most of the neighborhoods bored him. But this time Mr. Sweeny had promised something special. Today Jeremiah would see the Parthenon, the

Acropolis, and, miles away on the horizon, the Aegean Sea.

Jeremiah was out of breath. Clinging to a branch as he rested for a moment, he caught a murmur from the window to his left. His hands tensed around the branch. His lips curled into the private smile he had smiled for fifty years, each time he overheard something he had not been meant to hear, up in the cedar tree.

"I never make mistakes," said Mr. Sweeny.

"Oh, dear!" said Mrs. Sweeny. "Couldn't you call it a miscalculation? Because no one, not even the youngest children, will believe we are in Greece, and you promised us, you know."

"I never miscalculate, and I didn't promise," said Mr. Sweeny.

He coughed. Jeremiah waited while the cough grew from an irritated rasp into a lengthy rumble, like approaching thunder.

"You mentioned the Acropolis," said Mrs. Sweeny.

"That could mean anything."

"Homer and Sophocles. There's no denying you spoke of Homer and Sophocles."

"Both dead," said Mr. Sweeny.

"I'd be quite willing to believe you, dear," his wife said doubtfully. "I can't speak for the others, though. They're sure to wonder, and the children will be disappointed, especially Jeremiah. He's a sweet little thing, although he tends to whine a bit too much, and he's been begging for this trip ever since his mother started him on ancient Greece.''

"It won't do him a mite of harm to be thwarted for once in his life. He gets his way too often, living alone with his mother. Spare the rod and spoil the child!''

Mrs. Sweeny sighed. Jeremiah thought he could feel the sigh as it rippled past the white lace curtains out the window.

"Goodness knows you've spoiled us all,'' she said. "We've been around the world without leaving home, so to speak. Still, this time you made a mistake, and you'd better face it. Why not blame the windchill factor, or acid rain, or the Common Market? Blame anything you like, but admit we're not where we aimed to be and have done with it. After all, you're only human.''

"I'm never *only* anything!'' Mr. Sweeny roared. "I am in great distress, and you stand there insulting me.''

He coughed again. This time the cough seemed endless. Jeremiah could hear the creaky springs of the armchair where Mr. Sweeny had sat day after day for fifty years, blankets tucked around his portly body as he directed the affairs of Pineapple Place.

"I'm growing old,'' said Mr. Sweeny, suddenly resigned.

His wife's voice became brisk. "Nonsense, dear. We none of us ever grow. Not old, nor up and down, nor in and out. You're just tired from the move.''

"I'm feeling poorly, all the same.''

"Motion discomfort," said Mrs. Sweeny. "Chronic cyclical anticipatory motion discomfort. You have it for days before each move we make, and now you're feeling the aftereffects."

"Better call a general meeting," Mr. Sweeny said in a voice that oozed with self-pity. "Get the children in here, too. I'll take your advice and say it was a miscalculation. I'll apologize. Or better yet, I'll resign. How's that for an idea? O'Malley could take over my job, or Anderson, or Todd."

"Nonsense!" said his wife. "How could you suggest such a thing? Why, we owe you our very lives! We owe you the gift of eternal youth!"

"Or eternal old age, in the case of some of us," Mr. Sweeny groaned.

"Nonsense," his wife repeated firmly. "Now, you just sit back and relax while I fetch the Epsom salts."

Jeremiah took a deep breath and continued toward his secret place. He climbed carefully, because the bark was rough and left itchy pink welts on his skin that his mother was sure to notice. At last, safely wedged between the trunk and the crook of two branches, he peered over the familiar rooftops of Pineapple Place.

There was Mrs. Pettylittle with her shopping bags. She always went to work early on arrival days and came home laden with supplies. Her bags didn't look full yet. Jeremiah was surprised. Why would she have trouble in a city like Athens?

But this didn't look much like a city. In fact, he

could see only one building. It was a white, wood-frame house with green shutters, and gables above the upstairs windows. The house was set in a square of tidy lawn. A bicycle was lying on the lawn, and a golden retriever lay beside it. There were elm trees to the right, an asphalt driveway to the left. A Ford station wagon was parked in front of a two-car garage. Beyond the lawn, the house, the trees, was a slice of blue water. Jeremiah didn't think it was the Aegean Sea.

Closing his eyes briefly, he remembered the words he had read year after year in his fourth-grade textbook: "Stark, white limestone bluffs, dusty green olive orchards, and the clear, blue sea."

But they were not in Greece, or anywhere else in Europe. They were in a suburban town, and Jeremiah guessed it was on the coast of New England. Pineapple Place had been to many towns like this, and they all seemed the same to him. How long would they stay this time—a year? Two years? Was Mr. Sweeny's talk of Athens nothing but a cruel joke?

Recklessly, hardly caring where he put his feet, he slid down from the cedar tree and hurried toward his home across the street. His shirt was ripped. Would his mother be upset? It was hard to tell, because he had never ripped his shirt before. All these years he had been the good one. The other children in Pineapple Place were continually up to mischief, but Jeremiah had never given a moment's trouble. "What's come over you?" his mother would ask.

If something had come over him, it was Mr. Sweeny's fault for not taking them to Greece as he had promised. Mrs. Sweeny had spoken of eternal youth. Who needed eternal youth if it meant eternal boredom? She had told her husband that the people in Pineapple Place never grew—not old, nor up and down, nor in and out—but something was growing in Jeremiah all the same. He suspected it was boredom.

2

"What's come over you?" Mrs. Jenkins asked.

She tucked in the torn cloth and lined the edges up again, carefully matching the pattern. "You've never been one to tear your clothes. Why, this must be the first time in your life!"

"And it's been an awfully long life," said Jeremiah.

"You can thank your lucky stars for that," his mother said. "Hand me the scissors, there's an angel. Who else has enjoyed fifty years of childhood, to say nothing of the nine before Pineapple Place first moved from Baltimore? Should I use blue thread, or green? It's so hard to know, with plaid."

"April has, and the O'Malley kids, if you can call it enjoying," said Jeremiah. "What's enjoyable about being nine for fifty years? Use any color you like. I couldn't care less.''

"Couldn't care less!" Mrs. Jenkins looked up from her mending. Her eyes—eyes like Jeremiah's, dark blue, fringed with dark lashes, in a pale face—widened anxiously. "Darling, are you feeling poorly?"

"I'm feeling bored," said Jeremiah. "I'm bored of Pineapple Place, and bored of myself. I'm bored of being a sweet little thing, although I tend to whine a bit too much."

"Who said that?" his mother asked sharply.

"Never mind. I'm bored of April, and I'm bored of the O'Malley kids, all five of them."

"April Anderson is a nice girl," Mrs. Jenkins said, biting the green thread and twisting the end into a knot. "Those O'Malleys are a rough-and-tumble lot, though— I'll agree with that. Did Mike O'Malley tear your shirt?"

"Oh, Mother!" Jeremiah slouched across the room and scowled at his image in the mirror. It annoyed him that even scowling he couldn't make his dimples disappear. "Want to know what it's like?" he asked. "It's like being a prisoner. I'm a prisoner in Pineapple Place, and it's not as if I committed a crime, so why can't I get out and live like real people?"

Mrs. Jenkins stitched quietly, joining the sides of the tear. "We're real enough ourselves," she said at last. "We lead a pleasant life, all in all. There must be something in particular that's bothering you."

Jamming a thumb into each dimple, Jeremiah raised

the outsides of his eyebrows with his forefingers and stuck out his tongue. The result, in the mirror, was a naughty cherub. Not bad, just naughty. "Do you realize where we are?" he demanded.

"Of course, dear. I took a stroll this morning, while you were still asleep. So quaint and pretty! Mr. Sweeny has done it again."

"Again?" Jeremiah's face puckered, and tears welled in his eyes. "Quaint and pretty? But he said we'd go to Greece. I've been learning about Greece for fifty years, and he promised. He said we'd see the Parthenon, and the Acropolis, and the Aegean Sea. I saw water out there, but it wasn't the Aegean Sea."

"It was Long Island Sound," Mrs. Jenkins said. "Now, don't get upset. You know how Mr. Sweeny likes to have his little joke, and wherever he takes us, he has his reasons. You're going to love it here."

"Where's 'here'?" asked Jeremiah.

"Athens, Connecticut." Mrs. Jenkins took one last stitch and snipped the thread. "There, it hardly shows. I want you to dress nicely while we're here. We're most of us respectable people, and if ever you have the misfortune to be seen, I'd like the outside world to know it. This is a privileged community: good families, no riffraff, and the school system is one of the finest in the country."

"So what?" said Jeremiah. "It could be one of the worst in the country and it wouldn't make any difference. We get taught by *you*, right here in Pineapple Place.

Fifty years of fourth grade! Fifty years of three-digit division and ancient Greece! I was so sick of ancient Greece I thought I'd throw up, until Mr. Sweeny promised we could move to Athens."

"It would have been modern Greece, in any case," his mother reminded him. "New England is much healthier."

"I bet it isn't, but that's not the point. The point is, you have no idea how boring it is to have the same fourth-grade teacher all your life—and she's your mother."

His mother looked hurt. "But you and Jessie know more than any other fourth graders in the world! Take geography, for instance. You're way ahead in geography, and learning more every day. Think how useful that is, given the circumstances."

"Why?"

"Well, what other children could wake up one morning to find their street had moved to Gdansk, and know that it was on the Baltic Sea?"

"What's useful about that?" Jeremiah asked. "We'd be there whether we knew what it was called or not. Knowing names isn't useful; it's boring."

Mrs. Jenkins frowned and folded the mended shirt. "Maybe I should move you up to fifth grade. I suppose you could handle the work."

"Of course I could," Jeremiah said. "I can do all the work, even in sixth grade, like the twins. What do you expect when we've been working together in the same room for half a century?"

His mother ignored the question. "The problem is, Jessie would want to move up, too. She wouldn't care to stay back in fourth alone. They'd all want to go into the next grade, but if Tessie and Bessie are in seventh, that means algebra. I'm not sure I remember any algebra."

Jeremiah sighed. "Never mind. It would make too much trouble, and it wouldn't change a thing. I wish something would really change. I wish I could be seen."

"Seen? Whatever next!" Mrs. Jenkins gave her head a shake that loosened her bun of thin, dark hair and sent a hairpin skittering across the floor. "Pick that up for me, there's a good boy. You must be careful not to drop or spill anything today. Mr. O'Malley hasn't quite finished hooking up the electrical wires so I can't use the Hoover yet, and you know how I hate to fuss with brooms."

Jeremiah made a sympathetic face, but secretly he was glad about the Hoover. His mother loved labor-saving devices and there was rarely a moment when he couldn't hear the whir of the sewing machine, the roar of the Hoover, or the startling buzz and snap of the toaster he once found for her in the trash. Moving days provided a welcome change. Mr. O'Malley, who serviced the household appliances, was also responsible for hooking up the current each time Pineapple Place moved to a new neighborhood, and the Jenkins house rested in silence until his work was done.

"It wouldn't matter if I did spill something for once," he pointed out. "I could just walk around it."

His mother's eyebrows shot up in dismay. "Over my dead body!"

"I could walk around that, too," said Jeremiah.

One look at his mother's face made him regret the joke. "I just meant, I can see you. It's not as if you died in the outside world. Then you'd be invisible, and people would trip over your dead body. You wouldn't like that, would you?"

Mrs. Jenkins smiled and shook her head. "It's not a pleasant subject of conversation, dear. I've always found it so upsetting that Mr. Sweeny couldn't make our invisibility one hundred percent reliable. Why, a person can't relax! But at least you've kept out of trouble all these years. I'm sure the O'Malleys are green with envy. Now, pick up that pin, and no more nonsense."

Dropping to his hands and knees, Jeremiah fished the hairpin from under the chest of drawers. His hand came out clean: not a fleck of dust. There wasn't a fleck of dust in the whole house. His mother told him repeatedly that the O'Malleys were green with envy about that, too, but Jeremiah didn't think they minded dust any more than they minded trouble.

"Invisibility has been a blessing to us all these years," his mother continued. "If we weren't invisible, people would notice us and wonder."

"Mrs. Pettylittle is visible," Jeremiah argued. "People see her all the time. She even talks to people, and they don't wonder."

"That's where you're wrong," his mother said.

"They do wonder, but she's a bag lady and it's normal to wonder about a bag lady. I don't know how we'd survive without Mrs. Pettylittle, but I wouldn't have her job for all the money in the world. Imagine poking through trash your whole life long, and decent people watching you do it. I'd faint from shame!"

Jeremiah wriggled impatiently; his mother was getting off track. "I think she's lucky," he insisted. "April and the O'Malley kids are lucky, too. They've been seen lots of times since Baltimore, and they never know when it might happen again. Why not me?"

"Because they're a bunch of scamps and you're a good boy." Mrs. Jenkins moved to the mirror, twisted her bun more tightly against her scalp, and secured it with the hairpin. "You're being very silly, and I don't want to hear another word. If you were seen I think it would break my heart, so mind you remain invisible. Is that clear?"

"Yes, Mother," Jeremiah said dully.

3

There was a nip in the air. Not in open places where the sun felt like a warm bath, but under the trees where birches had brightened into yellow and maples into crimson with smudges of green.

New England was famous for this, Jeremiah knew. It was the season when leaves turned fancy and were called foliage. The trees looked like a calendar photo for October, and the old-fashioned, white wood houses fitted right in.

Jeremiah moved quickly with the peculiar gait that, he had discovered, got him farther faster than an outright run. He trotted several steps, slowed into a walk, speeded up with a little skip, and trotted again. There were few cars in the street and even fewer people on the sidewalk. He was relieved, since he lived in dread of jostling a passerby. He may never have been seen or heard but, like the others in Pineapple Place, he could be felt when he went into the outside world. A fat woman had once sat on his lap in the subway, and he had never forgotten the fuss she made.

As he hurried along, he looked anxiously over his shoulder toward the spot between two houses where Pineapple Place had settled the night before. Had the others seen him leave? Were April and the O'Malley kids stalking from bush to bush on these well-groomed lawns, ready to pop out and tease him?

Year after year he had played with them, even though he knew they thought of him as the sissy of Pineapple Place. All the children in Pineapple Place knew each other inside out, and often shared the same feelings without having to put them into words. Did April Anderson and the O'Malley kids feel what he was feeling now? Were they disappointed and bored after this latest move?

Jeremiah passed into the shade again and shivered. He didn't dare share his thoughts with the others, at least not yet. And he didn't want them to know where he was going that morning.

Somewhere in this town was an elementary school. Hadn't his mother told him Athens had one of the finest school systems in the country? Somewhere among these proper New England homes stood a red-brick building with an American flag in front. It was just a matter of tracking it down.

The first five blocks were all the same: big white

houses, smooth green lawns, and at the end of every driveway a mailbox with a picture of a cardinal on it, or flying ducks. Then the neighborhood changed and the houses grew smaller, closer together. Jeremiah could see a whole family's wash pegged up ear to ear on a backyard line. The front yards were strewn with strollers, plastic wading pools, tires planted with geraniums. There was even a bathroom sink toppled over on its side, waiting either to be installed or hauled away.

Jeremiah felt more comfortable here. He smiled, thinking how it reminded him of the O'Malleys' front yard, the only messy spot in Pineapple Place. Then he grew sober as a new thought struck him. Was it possible that, in spite of his mother, he was beginning to like mess?

The dogs were different in this neighborhood, too. They were scruffier and of no special breed. One came toward him now, wagging its tail.

Jeremiah stood still. He was afraid of dogs. Not that they ever growled or snapped at him: on the contrary, they seemed to like him. They would jump up and lick his face, and often knocked him over. When this happened, no one ever came to help. What owner would call his dog off someone he couldn't see?

"Go away!" Jeremiah commanded in a voice that was meant to sound firm, but came out shaky. "Go home!"

The dog sat down and grinned.

"Please go home, there's a good boy." He flushed, realizing how much he sounded like his mother.

The dog twisted around to worry a flea under a raised back leg.

"All right then," said Jeremiah. "If you won't go, I will."

He turned and started back. The dog stood up, shook all over with a clattering of tags, and followed. Suddenly a screen door banged open and shut as two more dogs hurtled into the street. They sniffed the first dog, circling cautiously. Then they sniffed at Jeremiah. Wagging their tails approvingly, they trotted at his side. At the end of the next block, where the fancy neighborhood began, they were joined by three golden retrievers and a black Labrador.

Jeremiah groaned. Why did dogs notice the children from Pineapple Place when people couldn't? Was it something to do with a dog's sense of smell, or was it just another of Mr. Sweeny's jokes? If so, it didn't make him laugh. On the contrary, he found it humiliating.

Unwilling to be escorted home by seven dogs, Jeremiah turned down a side street in the direction where, earlier that morning, he had caught a glimpse of Long Island Sound. After a block or so he found a small grocery store and a laundromat. A little farther was a low, bus-shaped structure with a sign that said FLO'S ACROPOLIS DINER. Jeremiah's mouth watered as he thought of gyros and souvlaki, but from what he could see through the window, the customers were eating hamburgers and fries.

This must be the commercial part of town, he

thought. He passed three liquor stores, a row of dress shops, a bank, and a delicatessen. All were closed. Then came a shop called GREEKS BEARING GIFTS. It was closed, too, but looking through the window, Jeremiah saw shelves of knickknacks, kitchen gadgets, and coffee mugs marked I ♡ ATHENS.

After the gift shop came the Parthenon Playhouse—a movie theater, Jeremiah gathered from the posters outside—and then Kourides' Pharmacy. Pharmacies stayed open when other stores were closed, Jeremiah knew. He pressed his face to the window and was attracted by a hand-printed sign that read

DON'T POISON YOUR CHILD!
Commercial Remedies Do More Harm Than Good
TRY NATURE'S WAY
Cure Your Child's Cough with
HOREHOUND, COLTSFOOT, and CHERRY BARK

Under the sign was a glass jar half-full of an oily, pea-green liquid. Jeremiah tried to see beyond to the back of the store but the sun was behind him, so instead he saw his own reflection in the window, floating palely among a display of tanning lotions. He stopped to practice the face he had made earlier that morning. He tried the door, but it was locked.

Walking to the next corner, he waited for the traffic light to change, and crossed to a train station. The station was locked, too. Athens, Connecticut, seemed sleepy today. Jeremiah wondered if it was sleepy all the time. And where was the school?

It was annoying to have no contact with people of the outside world. There were so many questions he wanted to ask! Sometimes he planned ways to ask them, but he had never dared put his ideas to the test. For instance, what if he went back to the Acropolis Diner and left a message on the counter? The message could say, "How do I get to the school? Please make a map."

The trouble was, things that the people in Pineapple Place wore or carried generally remained invisible until they were no longer touching them. Would Flo be frightened if she saw a piece of paper appear out of nowhere? Worse, would she guess he was there and try to grab him? He suspected he would never have the nerve to find out.

"Please make me brave!" he prayed silently. "Please, please make me brave, and make something happen!"

As if in answer to his prayer, he turned a corner and saw a red-brick building set in the middle of a grassy playground full of monkey bars, slides, and swings. Speeding up, followed by seven dogs, Jeremiah flung himself against the front door.

The door was closed. Closed and locked. If he had been going more slowly he would have noticed a sign thumbtacked to one of the panels. It said NO SCHOOL ON MONDAY: COLUMBUS DAY OBSERVED.

Jeremiah groaned with frustration. What was the

use of trying? he wondered. Today there was one reason and tomorrow there would be another, but the hard fact remained that nothing ever changed. On the verge of tears, he moved to a window and peered into a classroom.

Desks were grouped in little islands of four or six. Chairs had been turned upside down on top of the desks, leaving the floor space clear. All around the room, just under the ceiling, was a narrow frieze with the cursive alphabet in capitals and lowercase. Construction-paper cutouts decorated the walls: red and yellow maple leaves, black witches, orange jack-o'-lanterns. There was a full-length mirror on the opposite wall.

For the third time that day Jeremiah covered his dimples, distorted his eyebrows, and thrust out his tongue. Beside him, seven dogs stretched on their hind legs to claw at the windowsill, panting noisily. Suddenly another face appeared over his shoulder. It was the face of a girl a few years older than himself with big, pale-rimmed glasses and skinny, long, pale braids. The girl smiled at him in the mirror. Then she too jammed her thumbs into her cheeks, pulled up her brows with her forefingers, and stuck out her tongue.

Jeremiah turned and stared, but the girl paid no attention. Still looking in the mirror, she moved closer to the window and pressed her face against the pane. "Who's in there?" she shouted. "It's no use hiding. I saw you."

The dogs scattered as a man came hurrying around

the corner of the school. He jingled as if he too were wearing a collar with metal tags. Jeremiah, backing away cautiously, noticed that the noise came from a key chain clipped to the belt loop of his paint-stained jeans.

"Was that you making all that racket, Ruby? What's the problem?"

"There's someone inside there," the girl said. "I saw him, and there were all these dogs looking in the window at him, too, except I scared them away. He was making faces."

The man craned his neck, trying to see into all four corners of the classroom. "Nobody in there now. Not unless he's hiding in the closet. Who was he making faces at—you?"

"At himself in the mirror," Ruby said. "He wasn't doing anything bad. He just looked silly, and I wondered what he was up to in there."

"Can't think how he got there in the first place," the man said. "Everything's locked, except my room in the basement. I'd better take a look around. Want to come, Ruby?"

"No, thanks," she said. "I have to be back for lunch. How come you're working today, Mr. James? I thought you were on vacation, too."

"So I am," the man answered with a sheepish grin. "Problem is, this is the only place I can smoke a cigarette without the wife and kids bugging me about it. I promised them I'd kick the habit."

"Just so long as you don't smoke in Ms.

McAllister's classroom,'' Ruby warned him. ''It's bad for the guinea pigs.''

Selecting a large key from his chain, Mr. James unlocked the main entrance of the school and slipped inside. Ruby turned and walked away with the brisk pace of a hungry person who knows where to find a meal. Jeremiah was hungry, too. He thought longingly of the hot soup his mother always made for lunch on Mondays. But he wasn't ready to give up. Not when the thing he had hoped for had finally happened—or, with any luck, was about to happen.

Ruby had seen him in the mirror; he was sure of that. Why else did she imitate the face he made? Why else had she told Mr. James, who must be a janitor at Athens Elementary? She saw him in the mirror, but not in real life when she turned around. Still, it was better than nothing.

He followed Ruby back to the commercial street, not knowing what to do. If he touched her, she might scream. Besides, what then? He hadn't brought a pencil and paper to write her a message. If only he could find another mirror!

When Ruby reached the train station, she crossed the street. Not at the corner, waiting for the light as Jeremiah had, but right smack in the middle. Cringing at the thought of what his mother would say if she caught him jaywalking, Jeremiah looked quickly left and right, and then crossed, too.

It was obvious where she was headed: Kourides' Pharmacy. Didn't she know the pharmacy was closed?

He hurried now, curious to see if Ruby would try to go inside.

She didn't. At the last moment she turned toward another door, to the left of the pharmacy. Jeremiah guessed that this second door led to the apartment over the store. Just as Ruby reached out for the knob, he reached out and pulled one of her braids.

She didn't scream. She didn't even turn around. Instead she stared at her reflection in the pharmacy window. There was her face with its glasses and braids, and there was Jeremiah. Jeremiah smiled. After a moment's hesitation, Ruby smiled, too. Then she turned around.

"You weren't in the classroom after all," Ruby said. "Unless you live in mirrors, that is."

Jeremiah went on smiling. He wished he had a pencil and paper, to write a message back.

"You have some nerve!" said Ruby. "If I were invisible I'd keep away from people, but you've been following me, haven't you? You must be brave."

Jeremiah's smile grew broader. He liked this girl. He had always thought that if he were lucky enough to find a friend in the outside world he would want it to be a boy like him, but a boy would never call him brave. If only Ruby would look in his eyes when she talked! Instead she looked past his left ear, at the place she thought his eyes should be. Taking her by the shoulders, Jeremiah turned her toward the reflection.

"There you are again!" Ruby said. "Can you talk, or do you just make faces?"

Jeremiah sighed. Then he noticed his sigh misting

over the window glass of Kourides' Pharmacy and had an idea. Pointing his finger at the glass, he wrote "HELLO RUBY!"

Ruby laughed. "Hello, mirror boy. What's your name?"

Jeremiah pointed again and traced the letter *J*.

"Jay," said Ruby. "Is your name Jay?"

Jeremiah breathed on the window a second time to mist up a space large enough to finish writing *Jeremiah*, but the door swung open behind Ruby and a man appeared. He was dressed in brown from head to toe: a brown knit cap pulled over his ears, a brown tweed jacket, brown pants, and a pair of old brown slippers on his feet. At first Jeremiah thought he was very old. Then he decided that he just looked very tired. The man slouched a little, and tilted only one side of his mouth up when he smiled.

"How do you do?" he said. "May I be of assistance?"

He wasn't talking to Ruby, or to Jeremiah. Instead he focused, through pale-rimmed glasses like Ruby's own, at someone standing farther back. Jeremiah turned and found himself face to face with Mrs. Pettylittle.

"Go away!" he whispered. "Don't spoil it. She can't see me except in mirrors, but I think I'm finally making a friend."

Mrs. Pettylittle ignored him. She smiled back at the man in brown. "How kind of you, and how very timely! I was at my wit's end. Would you kindly direct me to the dump?"

"The Transfer Station, you mean," said the man in brown. "It's quite a walk from here: out Route one, then left on Colonial Lane, just past the lumberyard."

"You can't think how distressed I am," Mrs. Pettylittle murmured, looking sadly into her empty shopping bags. "The trash in this town is a terrible disappointment. But thank you, all the same."

"My pleasure. Feel free to return, if there's anything else I can do. Kourides is my name: Homer Kourides, and Ruby here is my niece."

Still slouching and smiling his tilted smile, Homer Kourides pulled Ruby inside and shut the door.

4

"Transfer Station," Mrs. Pettylittle murmured thoughtfully as she rearranged her hat in the reflection. "That's out beyond where we're installed. I saw a sign for it this morning, but I never guessed it meant the dump."

Jeremiah crossed his arms and scowled up at a second-story window. "You spoiled it," he said.

"I did no such thing, dear. That nice Mr. Kourides would have come down whether I was here or not. I could see him in that very window, looking for his niece. Was she a nice girl?"

Jeremiah shrugged.

"It makes a nice change for you, being seen, even if it was only in a mirror," Mrs. Pettylittle continued cozily. "I noticed she didn't look a bit afraid. I found such a nice, old-fashioned mirror the other day. Only one crack in the glass, and it has a silver handle. Would you like to bring it here and chat with her again?''

Jeremiah switched his scowl from the window to Mrs. Pettylittle. Ordinarily he liked the woman. She was cheerful and practical, and treated Jeremiah like an equal. She didn't seem cheerful today, however, and Jeremiah wasn't in the mood for liking anybody except Ruby, who was gone.

"No," he said. "What's the use? I can't chat because she wouldn't hear me, and I can't go on waving in mirrors. I was writing her a message when you turned up and spoiled things."

Mrs. Pettylittle nodded encouragingly. "That was a nice idea, dear."

Jeremiah lost his temper. "Nice, nice, nice! Nothing is nice. It's all terrible. I'm sick of being invisible, and I'm sick of being nine years old, and I'm sick of being a prisoner in Pineapple Place!"

He clenched his fists and squinched up his eyes, waiting for reproach. Mrs. Pettylittle would tell him he was lucky to be nine forever and travel all over the world without leaving his neighborhood. Her voice would be kind, and she would make him feel guilty.

To his surprise, her voice was cross. "I quite agree with you, Jeremiah. Not that I know what it is to be invisible. In fact, I often wish I were—it would make my work easier. And I'm not nine, of course. I'm fifty-seven. But if I had my choice of being a fifty-seven-year-old bag lady for the rest of time or not, I'd say

'Thank you, I'll take *not*.' Still, if it weren't for Mr. Sweeny, I'd be a hundred and seven. Every cloud has a silver lining!''

Content at last with the angle of her hat, she started walking in the direction of Pineapple Place. Jeremiah walked beside her. He almost offered to carry her bags, but saw they were still empty. Perhaps that was why she was upset.

"I always thought you liked rag-bagging," he said. "I thought it was fun."

"Fun for you," she grumbled. "You and April and those O'Malley rascals are always on the lookout for toys or whatnot. No one cares if you come home empty-handed. But it's my job, and I seem to be losing my touch."

"Didn't you find anything good?" Jeremiah asked, feeling friendlier again.

"Good? I didn't find anything at all. I've never salvaged a bit of yarn, however tangled, that Mrs. Anderson wasn't able to work into a sweater, or a scrap of paper that your mother couldn't turn to some use for her teaching. But today? Nothing!"

"That's too bad," Jeremiah said. "I suppose it's because we're in New England."

"New England?" Mrs. Pettylittle glanced at him in surprise. "What difference does that make? People throw trash out all over the world. Athens, Connecticut, or Athens, Greece."

"New Englanders are frugal," Jeremiah informed

her. "It says so in my mother's social studies book. It means Waste Not, Want Not. You know: wear it out, don't throw it out. Like us."

Mrs. Pettylittle burst out laughing. "Like us? These people? Look around you!"

Jeremiah had noticed only Ruby and her uncle, and the janitor at the Athens elementary school. Now he looked. Mrs. Pettylittle was right: the people in the street seemed well-to-do. Their clothes and shoes were new, their cars were new, their houses had newly shingled roofs and new coats of paint. Everything looked expensive. Nothing looked as if it had been put together with bits of other things that had been found in the trash.

"They've got more than they want, and you can bet your life they waste a good part of it," said Mrs. Pettylittle. "The point is, where does it go?"

They walked in silence past the shops, the bank, the liquor stores, and Flo's Acropolis Diner. They reached the fancy neighborhood. As usual, Jeremiah attracted a dog or two, but Mrs. Pettylittle shooed them away. They reached the spot where Pineapple Place had settled the night before.

"Here you are," Mrs. Pettylittle said, pausing for a moment.

Jeremiah looked down the familiar cobbled street with its ten old-fashioned brick houses, five on each side. He could hear voices: his mother calling from an upstairs window to Mr. Todd across the way. April's mother singing softly as she watered her geraniums. An

O'Malley girl yelling at her brother. He wasn't sure he wanted to go home.

"Where are you going?" he asked.

"To the Transfer Station, of course," said Mrs. Pettylittle. She gave a delicate shudder. "They can call it what they like, but to me a dump is a dump, and I never thought the day would come when I'd be obliged to work in one."

Jeremiah had never been to a dump, but he could imagine what it was like. "Why not? All the good stuff would be in one place, so you wouldn't lose time going around the streets."

"I prefer the streets, thank you," Mrs. Pettylittle snapped. "At least you're sure where your trash comes from. When it's all jumbled together, you never know. But today I have no choice. If the trash flow stops, what will become of Pineapple Place?"

"You could buy what we need, like ordinary people," Jeremiah suggested.

She shook her head gloomily. "Mr. Sweeny took a million dollars in cash when we left Baltimore, back in '39. That's a lot of money, but it's not going to last forever, and it looks as if we are. It's to be used for food, and food only. Anything else must be salvaged from the trash."

Still shaking her head, she produced the list she had tucked into a glove, just over her left wrist. " 'Lag bolts, flatheads, and dowel screws.' That's for Mr. Todd. How am I supposed to tell the difference? If I see a screw I'll take it, and he can decide what kind it is. 'Rubber spatula.' That's for your mother. Hope springs eternal! She's put it on the list for years, but I've never found her one. 'Yarn' for Mrs. Anderson, as usual. 'Strap hinge, split-wing toggles, and a jamb-nut adapter' for Mr. O'Malley. I don't even know what they are! He claims his house was unduly shaken during the move, but if you ask me, it's those children who shake the house. One day they'll bring it down over his head.''

Mrs. Pettylittle looked tired. Her veil had gone limp, and little wrinkles had appeared at the sides of her mouth. Jeremiah felt sorry for her.

''Why do you do this?'' he asked. ''Why do any of us do it? We should just go into stores and get what we want, without all this poking around in the trash. We could take a spatula, and yarn, and split-wing toggles, too.''

Mrs. Pettylittle raised her eyebrows and fixed him with a cold stare. ''Stealing, that's what you mean, isn't it? Shoplifting and getting away with it because no one can see you?''

Jeremiah had prepared an argument that he hoped would convince her once and for all. ''When we're holding onto a thing, it disappears for the people in the outside world, right? Well, if they can't see it any-more—say it's a spatula, for instance—then as far as they're concerned, it isn't really there, and you can't steal something that isn't there, can you?''

Mrs. Pettylittle tucked the list back into her glove.

"Stealing," she repeated firmly. "We've always managed honestly, and I hope we always will. Now, how about helping me this morning? Run in and get the others, too. Many hands make light work."

Jeremiah's face clouded. "I'd rather come alone."

The rag-bag lady looked shrewdly into his eyes. "What's up? You're not quite yourself today."

"You mean, not so sweet, although I tend to whine a bit too much?"

Mrs. Pettylittle laughed. "Did you have an argument?"

"Not yet," said Jeremiah. "I mean, I'm in the sort of mood where I might. I feel so different today, and I'd like to go on feeling different, but the others always expect me to be the same, so I'll probably just—"

"—slip back into the role." Mrs. Pettylittle finished his sentence for him. "Well, it's hard to change when you're not allowed to grow, but it's certainly worth a try. Why not take my mirror back to town and make friends with that girl? And if you don't mind another tad of advice, talk to her."

"Talk to Ruby? What good would that do?"

"Who knows?" said Mrs. Pettylittle. "But I noticed that you didn't even try. Making faces, pulling braids—that's no way to find a friend! Open your mouth and introduce yourself. Say who you are."

Jeremiah felt foolish. "You think she might hear me? But I never could make myself heard before."

"Then make yourself heard now," said the rag-bag lady.

Jeremiah squared his shoulders and practiced: "Hello, Ruby! I'm Jeremiah Jenkins."

It sounded good. He grinned, lifted his face to the blue October sky, and shouted, "Hey, Ruby! Hey, anybody out there! You want to know my name?"

"No," said a familiar voice.

He should have known that an outburst like that would bring the others running. April, with her quiet manners and her slightly mocking smile. The redheaded O'Malleys, who had no manners at all and made fun of him whenever they didn't have anything better to do, and sometimes even when they did. They were all there, all six of them.

Jeremiah let his breath out. He felt the air leaving his body: buckets and buckets of air escaping, as if he were a giant balloon and Mike had just deflated him. Because the voice could only have been Mike's. The girls teased and giggled, but only Mike knew how to devastate Jeremiah with a single word.

No one would dream of saying that Mike O'Malley was a sweet little thing. First, he wasn't sweet. Friendly sometimes, but not sweet. Second, he was hardly little. Only a year older than Jeremiah, he was a good four inches taller, and stockily built.

"Why should we want to know your name?" asked Mike O'Malley.

"I wasn't talking to you," Jeremiah muttered.

Mike opened his eyes with unconvincing innocence. "You weren't? But you said 'anybody.' Aren't I anybody?"

"Oh, leave him alone," said April Anderson. "You'll only make him cry. Have you been out already, Jeremiah?"

Of all the others, Jeremiah got along with April best. She could be bossy in her quiet way but she never bullied him, and she was fair. He ignored the O'Malleys and appealed to her. "Do you know what's happened, April? Mr. Sweeny took us to the wrong place. We're not where we're supposed to be at all."

"We're in Athens, Connecticut," April told him firmly, "and that's just where he intended us to go. That business about Greece was a joke. He called us into his house while you were gone and told us so."

"He's mad at you," five-year-old Meggie informed him solemnly. "He said you had no business going out alone. Not the first morning."

"You have to admit it was a sneaky thing to do," said one of the twins. "We always go together the first time. We agreed."

"Especially this time," the other twin added. "Mr. Sweeny says this is like a game. Those things he talked about—Homer, and the Parthenon, and the Acropolis—they're all out there, only it's Connecticut, not Greece, and we're supposed to find them."

Jeremiah remembered Flo's Diner, and the movie theater, and Ruby Kourides' uncle. He smiled his secret smile. "It's too late," he said. "I've already found them. The early bird gets the worm."

Meggie, the youngest of the O'Malley clan, crinkled her eyes and wailed. Mike just laughed. "Well, I take it they're still there to find. Unless you've got them in your pocket, or in Mrs. Pettylittle's shopping bags. So you can go home to your mama and the rest of us will explore."

"Oh, no, you won't!" said the rag-bag lady. "You're coming with me to the dump. Pardon me— Transfer Station. There's a trash-flow problem, and I need all the help I can get."

April's face lit up. "The dump? I thought you disapproved of dumps. Button your sweater, Meggie; it's chilly this morning. And Jessie, tie your shoelaces or you'll trip over them. Ready, everyone? This is going to be fun!"

A voice called from an upstairs window in the bluebrick house with yellow shutters—the second house on the right, going into Pineapple Place. "Jeremiah!"

Mrs. Pettylittle glanced up at the window, then back down at Jeremiah with a twinkle in her eye. "If you want to come with us, you'd better come now."

Jessie giggled. "She's right. Hurry up, Jeremiah, or your mama will get you, and you'll have to sit at home all day."

"Je-re-mi-aaah!" called the voice. "Answer me, there's a good boy!"

Jeremiah looked at the other children from Pineapple Place. They were smiling now. As usual, he couldn't tell whether they were teasing him or on his side. "That was my mother," he said unnecessarily.

April shrugged, bent down, and pulled up her socks. Meggie buttoned her sweater. Jessie and the twins were frowning over Mrs. Pettylittle's rag-bagging list. Should he go with them, or stay at home? Home was dull, but if he went with them he might be teased. He looked at Mrs. Pettylittle for encouragement, but she was too concerned with the trash-flow problem. He looked at Mike. Was Mike's smile friendly, or was it just a smirk?

His courage failed him. "That was my mother. I have to go."

In a desperate attempt to look casual, he sauntered up the walkway to his house, tripped on the top step, and fell through his own front door.

When he picked himself up, he saw that his shirt was torn again: split wide open at the seam his mother had so carefully stitched only a few hours earlier.

"Jeremiah, is that you?" his mother called.

Jeremiah turned and ran so fast that he caught up with the others half a block away.

5

"Go on ahead and I'll join you later," Mrs. Pettylittle told the seven children from Pineapple Place. "For the moment, I'm under the eye of the law."

She winked at them before turning to flick her fingers cheerily at Officer Rossotti, who had just pulled up outside the entrance to the Transfer Station. "Good morning, Officer! Isn't it a perfect morning for a walk? Simply perfect!"

Jeremiah wished she didn't twitter quite so much when she was nervous. It embarrassed him.

"If you're visiting the area, I can tell you some better places to walk," said Frank Rossotti. "There's a colonial blacksmith shop down the road a bit, for instance. Not much going on here at the dump."

Mrs. Pettylittle waved her black-gloved hand at an official sign that had been fastened to the fence near the entrance. "Resources Recovery Authority, Athens Transfer Station, Volume Reduction Center," she read aloud in tones of awe. "How elegant! Everything so efficient and organized. We don't have anything like it back home."

Frank Rossotti leaned out the patrol car window and squinted in the sunlight. "Where's home?"

"Baltimore."

"And where do you keep your trash in Baltimore?"

"In trash cans, of course." The rag-bag lady smiled innocently. "Did you say a colonial blacksmith shop? Isn't that nice!"

"It isn't a bit nice," April grumbled as she led the others up the drive. "Why doesn't she come? There are plenty of other people here, and that policeman doesn't seem to mind. Real people, from the town. They call it recycling; I read about it in a newspaper once. That's what makes it respectable, so why can't Mrs. Pettylit-tle—"

She stopped and doubled over. "Stitch in my side!" she gasped.

"Serves you right for talking too much," Bessie said, and giggled.

The O'Malley girls always let April take the lead, even though the twins were older. They seemed quite happy to stand back and criticize. Usually Jeremiah liked to hear them, as he thought April was too bossy, but today he felt like contradicting everybody, no matter what they said.

"It's not just the policeman," he told April. "She and I have friends in this town. We have to keep up appearances."

The other children stopped in their tracks to stare at him. Their reactions were mixed. Bessie giggled again and was joined by her sisters. April's face had a look of disbelief that Jeremiah found insulting.

"The secret life of Jeremiah Jenkins!" Mike teased. "Appearances? That's a good one! I thought you specialized in *dis*appearances. You're the only one of us who has never been seen, except by that boy in Georgetown."

Jeremiah was torn. Should he tell, or should he keep his secret? He was proud of going to Athens Elementary and meeting Ruby, but for the time being he wanted to keep her to himself. He decided to play it safe.

"Never mind," he said.

"Then don't hint," said Mike. "It's just a form of boasting. Besides, we've got work to do. Who's taking what?"

"I'll do toys and magazines," April answered promptly, "and Meggie's going to help. The twins and Jessie are going over to plastic containers, and then maybe aluminum. That leaves appliances for you boys, unless you prefer to start with furniture."

"Appliances," Mike decided. "Mr. Todd said if I found the right parts, he'd put together a stereo."

The twins gaped at him enviously. "Just for you, or for all of us?"

"For me. I asked first."

"But if we find the parts, you'll have to share."

Mike's response was a tantalizing grin.

"Forget it," Tessie told Bessie, turning her back on her brother so swiftly that her skirt whipped around her knees. "Even if he gets a stereo, where will he get the records? He's just showing off. Let's go."

"Smart ass!" Mike yelled after her.

He stood with his fists clenched until she was out of earshot. Then he sighed. "She's right about the records," he confessed to Jeremiah. "Some things you just can't make. Not even if you're my pa, or Mr. Todd."

Jeremiah watched as Mike leaned over and scooped up a handful of pebbles. He watched Mike flip the pebbles at an abandoned air-conditioning unit. He also watched the faces of the townspeople who had heard the ping. Usually this kind of prank made him laugh hysterically. Today it didn't.

"Quit fooling around and tell me what we're looking for," he said.

Mike shrugged. "A turntable, for starters. Then we'll need a capstan, standoff insulators, phone jacks, pressure rollers, and a thing called a stylus. We may not find everything today, but we'll get it together eventually. Remember, we have all the time in the world."

All the time in the world. But whose world? Their own inside world where nothing ever changed. Jeremiah couldn't work up much enthusiasm for it.

"Come on, let's get moving," Mike said, thrusting his arm up to the elbow into a heap of rusty metal.

Jeremiah thrust his own slim arm into another heap of metal. He felt nut-shaped things and bolt-shaped things. He also felt a sharp pain in his wrist.

Little drops of blood darkened the earth like drops of rain. Two of them fell, then half a dozen more.

"Are you okay?" Mike asked, eyeing the scratch doubtfully.

"I don't know." Jeremiah put his wrist to his mouth and licked it. He could almost hear his mother's horrified reaction. If he ran home she would clean the scratch and bandage it. He was debating whether to leave the dump when he heard a little gasp behind him. Swinging around, he saw Ruby and Mrs. Pettylittle. Ruby's back was turned to Jeremiah, but her face was reflected in the mirror of a discarded medicine cabinet.

"You hurt yourself!" she said. "Why did you come here, mirror boy? Why are you and this lady so interested in the dump? I followed her here, and then I saw you just by chance."

Jeremiah didn't know what to do. He wanted so badly to keep Ruby to himself. After all, she was his first real outside friend in fifty years. If Mike found out, would he spoil things?

"Who's that?" Mike asked, as if he were reading Jeremiah's thoughts. "She acts as if she knows you, but why isn't she looking your way?"

Jeremiah hated himself for doing it, but his only

choice was to ignore her. "What are you talking about?" he said. "I never saw her before." Thrusting the scratched hand deep into his pocket, he walked quickly away to a place where there were no mirrors.

The Second Day

6

Jeremiah woke at dawn. He lay under the covers with his eyes still shut while his mind spun around like the ball in a roulette wheel and finally settled as he remembered where he was. Then he went back to sleep and dreamed of water.

The water was deep blue, frosted with sunlight. In his dream, Jeremiah knew it was the Aegean Sea. He swam easily under the surface and breathed the water like air. But the easy feeling turned to panic: a nameless threat made him hurry now, and in his haste, his muscles tensed and slowed him down. A noise slipped up behind him. Soon the noise was all around him, engulfing him. He drowned in noise. He cried out, trying to make his own noise heard over the drowning noise, and his cry woke him up a second time.

The noise continued: a shoving, and a scraping, and a lengthy rumble. It came from the room next door.

Jeremiah sat up. His ears still pounded from the dream that had turned into a nightmare, but he recognized the roar of the ancient Hoover that his mother had kept from the old days back in Baltimore, when she lived in normal time. This meant that Mr. O'Malley had finished hooking up Pineapple Place with the electrical currents of Athens, Connecticut. His mother would be in a better mood.

But why was she vacuuming at all? That room was clean. Jeremiah had retrieved a hairpin from under the dresser only yesterday and had noticed the total absence of dust. How much new dust could fall in one day?

He swung his legs over the side of the bed, moving stealthily so the bedsprings wouldn't creak. He placed his bare feet on the chilly wooden floor and stood up. He reached for the clothes his mother had left folded on a chair. Could he get dressed and slip out of the house before she knew he was awake?

No such luck. The Hoover stopped abruptly, like a startled animal that had scented danger. A door opened and footsteps echoed in the hall.

"Rested, dear?" his mother asked. "No trouble sleeping last night? The house is facing west this time. I find the change quite troublesome. I couldn't sleep a wink."

"Sorry," Jeremiah murmured automatically. He looked around for his shoes and socks.

"Oh, it's not your fault. Now, wash quickly and come down for a bite to eat. The other children will be here soon. I told them to come early, to make up for missing school yesterday."

"Yesterday would have been a holiday whether we moved or not," Jeremiah informed her. "It was Columbus Day Observed." He found his socks inside his shoes and began to pull them on his feet.

"Observed? Fiddlesticks!" Mrs. Jenkins snatched the socks away. Carrying them by the tips of the toes as if they might give her some disease, she dropped them into the hamper where she had told Jeremiah repeatedly to put his dirty clothes. "Newfangled nonsense, and I'll have no part of it. A date is a date and can't be moved this way or that."

"It's already been moved," Jeremiah said. "There's nothing you can do about it. There was a sign at the school yesterday that said Columbus Day Observed."

"A date is a date," his mother repeated firmly, "and I expect to see you at your desk at nine o'clock sharp. We're starting the chapter on Greek mythology today. That's always fun, isn't it?"

"No," said Jeremiah. "It was fun the first few times, but not the fiftieth. If we were in Greece the way Mr. Sweeny promised, it might be fun again."

A bowl of fruit and a plate of lightly buttered toast had been set out for him in the kitchen. Ignoring them, Jeremiah slipped into the street. It was only half past eight.

The air in Pineapple Place was thick with smells of breakfast. Mrs. Pettylittle's house, to his left, smelled of hot Danish pastry. The O'Malleys' house, to the right, smelled of oatmeal, slightly charred. Across the street, Mr. Todd was cooking his bachelor breakfast of bacon and eggs, and next door Mrs. Anderson was brewing coffee (unless it was Dr. Anderson, who liked to cook almost as much as he liked to experiment with chemicals, and sometimes brewed coffee on a Bunsen burner while he pursued his search for a cure for the common cold).

Jeremiah loved bacon and eggs, but his mother claimed they were indigestible first thing in the morning. He moved across the street and stood at Mr. Todd's kitchen window. The window was closed, but he pressed his nose against the glass and tried to look like a hungry waif.

Mr. Todd was fussing over a frying pan. His eyeglasses were misted over from the steam, and the bald patch on his scalp shone more pinkly than usual. There was a splinter of eggshell on his mustache. Jeremiah tapped on the glass pane, smiled a wistful smile, and waved.

Looking up abruptly, Mr. Todd dropped the fork and glared. Then he chuckled. He wiped his hands on the dish towel he had knotted around his waist and moved to the window. "Starving, are you? Don't tell me your mother doesn't feed you!"

Jeremiah cupped his hand behind his ear and raised his eyebrows, although he had heard quite clearly.

Mr. Todd hoisted the window up and leaned outside. "Quite the Oliver Twist, aren't you, Jeremiah! Too bad you have such a limited audience. You'd be a raving success in the moving pictures. Want some bacon?"

Jeremiah abandoned his waif look and grinned when Mr. Todd speared three strips of bacon and poked them out the window.

"Beautiful day!" Mr. Todd observed. "I always did like New England during this season. I grew up in Springfield, Massachusetts, you know. Went to school there as a boy. Mornings like this make me remember."

Jeremiah glanced over his shoulder toward the spot where Pineapple Place joined the outside world. He couldn't see the street, but he could hear children's voices.

"What time does school start?" he asked.

Mr. Todd looked at the kitchen clock. He looked at his wristwatch, and at a pocket watch that was attached to his trousers by a golden chain. He moved to the doorway and looked at a clock in the hall. Mr. Todd's house was full of clocks, each one of which he had made himself from bits of broken clocks and watches that Mrs. Pettylittle had retrieved from the trash.

"It's 8:51, right on the button," he said. "Schools generally start at 9:00. You'd better run along, or your mama will be over here hunting for you."

Jeremiah looked at him warily, wondering whether to confide in him or not. He decided to tell a little and keep a little back. "I'm not going to my mother's class today. I've got something else to do."

Mr. Todd didn't react the way some of the grown-ups in Pineapple Place would have reacted. He didn't ask if Mrs. Jenkins knew, or if any of the other children were going, too, or even where Jeremiah planned to go. He just nodded. "Playing hooky, are you? Got your lunch?"

Jeremiah shook his head. "I think you get free lunch where I'm going. Hot lunch, in a cafeteria."

"Better safe than sorry," said Mr. Todd. "Here, take an apple. How about a bacon sandwich? I've got more than enough bacon. And if I put some lemonade in a mason jar, will you remember to bring back the jar? Mrs. Pettylittle didn't find a single empty container yesterday. Can you believe it? Now, what else will you be needing for this escapade?"

Jeremiah thought. "Paper, maybe? Pencils?"

Mr. Todd looked in a cupboard and shook his head. "No paper. None that I can spare, anyway. And I'm running low on pencil stubs, but you're welcome to borrow one, so long as you return it."

Jeremiah could no longer remember the time back in Baltimore when jars and pencil stubs were tossed into the trash. For years now they'd been precious in Pineapple Place since they could be replaced only by long hours of searching through trash in the outside world. "Maybe I'll find some more today."

"Fat chance," Mr. Todd grumbled. "Mrs. Pettylittle says the folks here don't throw anything away. Not so much as an empty beer can, she says. Not that I have much use for beer cans, but what kind of a town is this, anyway?"

"A town with one of the finest school systems in the country," Jeremiah told him. "Thanks, Mr. Todd. And if anybody asks, don't tell them where I'm going, okay?"

"How can I tell what I don't know?" Mr. Todd answered. "Just take care you're not seen, that's all. Not that you've ever been one to get in trouble. You're such a little mama's boy, it's a wonder you're even skipping school, come to think of it."

Jeremiah boiled inside. "As a matter of fact, school is just where I'm going. And you can tell my mother, if you like. You can tell her that from now on I'm going to a real school with real people, instead of staying cooped up with a street full of fussbudgets."

Mr. Todd's mouth dropped open, and then tightened into a little round O. His eyes grew round, too. It would have been a comic face, if it hadn't looked so sad. In spite of his anger, Jeremiah noticed the sadness and felt ashamed.

"Sorry," he said. "It's just that I'm different now. At least, I'm going to start being different. So I wish you wouldn't—"

Mr. Todd interrupted him. "You can't."

"Yes, I can," said Jeremiah. "I found the school yesterday, and there's no reason why I shouldn't go. I have a right to be educated like all those kids outside, even if I happen to be invisible."

"*Educated*, maybe," said Mr. Todd. "*Different*, out of the question. It's a mixed blessing, I'll admit, but none of us will ever be one jot different from what we

53

were back in 1939, so it's no use trying. Visit a school if you like. Put an apple on the teacher's desk, but forget about being different. Remember, you're only young once.''

"Only young once!" Jeremiah repeated as Mr. Todd slammed his kitchen window shut again. "What happens when once is forever?''

He slipped the bacon sandwich into a jacket pocket and the mason jar of lemonade into another, but he threw Mr. Todd's apple in a long, high arc over the rooftops of Pineapple Place to the outside world.

7

By the time Jeremiah reached Athens Elementary School, he had collected three beagles and a cocker spaniel. The school doors had been propped open to let in the morning air. When he walked inside, the dogs followed. Their claws scraped and skidded over the linoleum floor, making a racket that brought teachers running from their classrooms. For once, Jeremiah was glad to be invisible.

While the teachers tried to herd the dogs outdoors again, Jeremiah slipped along the hallways looking for Ruby. He was relieved not to find her name on the lists posted outside the fourth-grade rooms. Although he wanted to be in her class, he didn't think he could bear another year of Vikings and three-digit division. Her name wasn't outside the fifth-grade rooms either. Jeremiah began to panic—maybe she went to another school. But he found her at last on a list marked MS. MCALLISTER'S SIXTH GRADE.

Jeremiah caught his breath. The O'Malley twins did American history in sixth grade, and problems involving fractions. Would he be able to keep up with Ruby's class? He was apprehensive, but reminded himself that it wasn't as if Ms. McAllister could see him and say he looked too young.

He walked into the room, stepping carefully and holding his elbows close to his sides to avoid bumping into anyone or anything. The students were sitting in groups of five or six at round tables. They seemed to be working on several different projects, and in spite of Ms. McAllister's exit to the hallway, they worked quietly.

Jeremiah wriggled out of his jacket and hung it on an empty hook with the other jackets at the back of the classroom. He pulled his sandwich and the mason jar of lemonade from the jacket pockets and set them on a shelf, but didn't notice any other lunches there. He must have guessed right about the cafeteria. Still careful not to attract attention, he moved toward Ruby's table and stood where he could watch what she was doing.

"Dogs!" Ms. McAllister announced as she returned and shut the door behind her. "Four of them. Odd, they seemed to want to come in here. Is one of you a canine pied piper?"

The sixth graders laughed, except for Ruby. Jeremiah noticed a stiffening of her shoulders, as if she remembered the dogs that had followed him to school the day before. Could she guess that he had come back? He wanted to nudge her, or kick her foot under the table, maybe even pull her braid again, but he forced himself to wait.

"Before we start our math lesson, I'm going to pass out your reports on class structure in the Middle Ages," Ms. McAllister announced. "They were pretty good, on the whole. Some were excellent. Michael Featherstone made a graph showing the distribution of thanes, thralls, and churls among the population. Mandy Costello made a beautiful diorama with costumes of the period. It's going to be part of our library exhibit. Ruby Kourides had an interesting idea: herbal remedies, and their use in the treatment of the terrible epidemics that swept through Europe. How about reading one of your recipes to the class, Ruby?"

Ruby bit her lip as she took the pages Ms. McAllister handed her. Then she smiled. Looking over her shoulder, Jeremiah saw that her report was marked with an *A* and a happy face. He jumped out of the way as Ruby shoved back her chair, stood up, and began to read.

" 'The bubonic plague, otherwise known as the black death, was a lot scarier than the diseases of our time,' " Ruby read. " 'Back in the Dark Ages, people didn't know where it came from. All they knew was that if they caught it, chances were they'd die a horrible death within three days. The way they knew they had it was they got repulsive pustules under their armpits and between their legs. Their skin turned black and blue, and their breath smelled really foul. They spat blood, and vomited, and—' "

Ms. McAllister put her hands up to her face and then let them drop weakly to her side again. "Ruby, dear, I didn't ask for the symptoms, I asked for the cure. And please bear in mind that we're still digesting breakfast."

Ruby blinked at the teacher through her pale-rimmed glasses before turning a page. "Sorry," she said. "There wasn't any cure for bubonic plague back then, but people used angelica, and asafetida, and mandrake root, of course. And they believed in the healing powers of rosemary and rue. The monks probably treated fever with masterwort, sticklewort, and pennyroyal—steeped in an infusion, equal parts. Oil of wormwood, but not more than a dozen drops a day, because wormwood is poisonous if you take too much. Rootstock of fraxinella, swallowed a spoonful at a time—and by the way, you have to watch out not to touch the plant, because it makes your skin break out unless you stay in the shade. Some herbalists thought powdered mugwort was a good febrifuge, but actually it did more harm than good. Personally, I'd say a tincture of chamomile would work better—"

A boy near the front of the room snickered and raised his hand. "How do you know?" he asked.

Ruby scowled. "What do you mean, how do I

know? I know because that's what my report was on, so I found out."

"I bet you made it up," the boy said. "Or you got it out of a fairy tale or something dumb like that." He turned toward the other students and grinned.

"Okay, how much do you want to bet?" asked Ruby.

Ms. McAllister intervened. "Hold it, kids! This is a classroom, remember? Jason's question was a good one. Any scientific work should list its sources, Ruby. Did you use *The World Book Encyclopedia?*"

"Not exactly," Ruby said. "I asked my uncle."

"She asked her uncle," Jason repeated, looking around the classroom with a meaningful smile. "You know—Try Nature's Way!"

The other sixth graders seemed embarrassed. Jeremiah thought Ms. McAllister looked embarrassed, too. In any case, she was quick to change the subject. Within seconds, the students had put their history reports inside their desks and were sitting with pencils and blank sheets of paper while their teacher wrote a series of math problems on the blackboard.

"You have until ten-thirty," she said cheerfully. "The important thing in this quiz is to show that you remember what we learned last week. It doesn't matter if you don't have time to finish, but each problem you do should be carefully worked out, showing the different steps you went through to get the answer."

She went on to remind the class that to add fractions with different denominators, they had to find equivalent fractions with the same denominator. It was just what Jeremiah's mother said when she talked about fractions, and the problems on the board were like the ones she had written out each Friday for fifty years when the O'Malley twins did their weekly math quiz. They looked so easy that he couldn't understand why Ruby sat frowning at the paper on her desk, gnawing the eraser end of her pencil.

Five minutes went by before Ruby made the slightest mark on the paper. Even then, it was only to copy the first problem:

$$11\tfrac{2}{3}$$
$$+\ 9\tfrac{3}{4}$$

She stared at the problem on the paper. Then she stared at the same problem on the board. At last she glanced down at her paper again, as if she hoped the problem had solved itself while she was looking away. Jeremiah felt sorry for her. He reached over her shoulder to pull the pencil from her hand.

The instant the pencil was in Jeremiah's hand, it disappeared. The marks it made on the paper were perfectly visible, though. Jeremiah wrote the steps of the problem down clearly, so that Ruby would know how to do the next one:

$$11\tfrac{2}{3} = 11\tfrac{8}{12}$$
$$+ \ 9\tfrac{3}{4} = \underline{\ 9\tfrac{9}{12}}$$
$$20\tfrac{17}{12}$$

$$20\tfrac{17}{12} = 20 + 1 + \tfrac{5}{12} = 21\tfrac{5}{12}$$

When he had finished, he laid the pencil on the table, where it became visible again. Quickly he looked at Ruby to catch the pleased expression on her face.

Ruby drew in her breath with a little hiss. She grabbed the piece of paper and crumpled it. For a moment, her face crumpled, too. It looked angry, not pleased. Jeremiah noticed tears in her eyes.

Ms. McAllister left her desk and walked quietly over to Ruby. "What's the matter?" she asked. "Why did you destroy your work? It never helps to lose your temper when you have a setback, Ruby. Let's see how you dealt with the problem, and what I can do to help. Then maybe next time you won't have any trouble."

Her voice was calm and pleasant as she smoothed out the ball of paper, but when she looked at the problem, it sharpened with surprise. "But this is correct, Ruby. See? You were wrong to give up so soon. You did a beautiful job, and you wrote the steps out neatly. What made you crumple it up?"

"Because it was cheating," Ruby said. "Never mind, what do you care? You don't want me in this class anymore. You don't even want me in this town anymore, so why pretend you care?''

She snatched the paper out of her teacher's hand, crumpled it up a second time, and threw it at a wastebasket as she ran out of the room.

8

Jeremiah was in too much of a hurry to be careful leaving the classroom. As he stumbled by the last table, he swept a pile of papers to the floor and knocked over a chair. He didn't stop to see if anyone noticed. All he thought of was Ruby. What had upset her, and where was she going?

He caught a glimpse of her pale braids flapping around a corner of the hallway and heard her sneakers squeaking on the polished floor. His own old-fashioned, leather-soled shoes slid precariously, as if he were running on ice. Nevertheless, he was right on her heels when she flung open the door to the largest bathroom Jeremiah had seen in all fifty-nine years of his life.

It was a bathroom, but there was no tub. Only a long row of sinks against one wall and, built against the other, a series of cubicles with swinging doors that didn't reach all the way to the floor. Inside each cubicle was a toilet. Jeremiah counted enough toilets for each child in Pineapple Place to have his own, with one left over.

When he tried the door to the eighth cubicle, at the far end of the room, he found it locked. A pair of feet was planted behind it. Glancing down at the space above the floor, he recognized Ruby's sneakers. Impatiently, he waited for her to come out. With that row of mirrors over the row of sinks, he could try to communicate and find out what was wrong.

Jeremiah lifted his hand to tap on Ruby's cubicle, but backed off quickly when the bathroom door swung open again and Ms. McAllister bustled in.

"Ruby?" she called.

Jeremiah slipped into an empty cubicle and sat with his legs drawn up on a toilet seat, in case Ms. Mc-Allister also had the gift of seeing him in mirrors.

"Ruby, dear, are you all right? Come out and talk to me."

Ruby remained where she was.

"I know this is a stressful time for you," Ms. McAllister continued softly. "Running away and hiding won't help, though. We need to share our problems. If you'd only talk things out, you'd come to understand how moving to your new family will be a positive experience—"

Jeremiah heard the squeak of Ruby's sneakers on the floor. Was she coming out? Was she still crying? Abandoning his usual caution, he stepped into the open.

Ruby's face was streaked and blotchy. Her eyes had turned the same brighter, greener blue that the O'Malley girls' eyes turned when they cried. The difference was that when the O'Malley girls cried, Jeremiah felt impatient, but he wanted to comfort Ruby.

A long strip of toilet paper dangled from Ruby's hand. She glared defiantly at Ms. McAllister before blowing her nose into it. Then she wadded it up and carefully wiped her eyes. A look of repulsion spread over Ms. McAllister's face, and Jeremiah burst out laughing.

From then on, there was trouble. Ms. McAllister's back was to the mirrors, and her expression did not change. But Ruby froze, turned to stare blindly in Jeremiah's direction, then turned again and saw him in the mirror.

"Why are you here?" she whispered.

Then she yelled. "Why did you come today? Who asked you to do my math? This is none of your business and this is a girls' room, so get out of here! Go away!"

Ms. McAllister bit her bottom lip and shook her head. "That's quite enough, Ruby," she said gently. "I know you're upset, but there's no call for rudeness. I think you'd better come with me."

Jeremiah gave them a few minutes' head start before returning to the classroom. This time, the room was empty. He supposed everyone had gone off for music, or art, or one of the other "extras" he knew were taught in public schools. Rather than track Ruby down a second time he took his jacket, his bacon sandwich, and his mason jar of lemonade out to a corner of the playground where he could keep an eye on the front entrance of the school.

An hour and a half passed by. Bells rang now and then, marking changes in schedule. Jeremiah heard children's voices rising shrilly after each bell, but he couldn't distinguish Ruby's voice among the others. A group of small children ran out to play, followed by two teachers. After a while another bell rang and they went back inside. Parents drove up from time to time, went into the school, and came out again with a child. The child was never Ruby.

Jeremiah grew bored. In his head, he reviewed the facts he had learned from Ruby's paper. "Repulsive pustules," he said to himself. "Foul breath. Masterwort, and sticklewort, and rootstock of . . . of what? Flax? No, flaxinella. No, that wasn't it. What was it?"

At his side, a dachshund grunted sympathetically and rolled over to be scratched. Several other dogs sat nearby on their haunches, panting and wagging their tails.

"Fraxinella," Jeremiah told the dachshund. "That was it—rootstock of fraxinella."

He scowled at the dogs. Some of them he recognized from the day before. Why couldn't they follow someone who was fond of dogs?

The dachshund gave him a reproachful look and in spite of himself, Jeremiah laughed. "I'd rather be friends with Ruby, but I may have to settle for a dog," he told the dachshund.

He was proud of feeling less afraid that day. Was he outgrowing his fear of dogs? And if he could grow out of something, didn't that prove Mrs. Sweeny and Mr. Todd were wrong to say the people in Pineapple Place couldn't change?

He reached out to stroke the dachshund. It didn't bite. He scratched behind its ears and it gave a moan of appreciation. "Good doggie," he said uncertainly. "Nice doggie. Friends, right?"

The dachshund growled. Jeremiah pulled his hand back quickly before realizing that it hadn't growled at him. It had growled at Ruby, who was shuffling across the playground in reverse, steering toward Jeremiah with the help of a little pocket mirror that she held just over her left shoulder. Jeremiah sprang to his feet and rushed to meet her.

"Watch it, Jay!" Ruby grumbled. "Don't knock me over. And call off your dogs, will you?"

"They're not my dogs, and my name's not Jay."

Ruby leaned down to pat the dachshund. "If it isn't Jay, what is it?"

Jeremiah began to say his name. Then he stopped and took a deep breath that ended in a howl of joy. "You heard me!" he shouted. "You can hear me!"

"So don't shout," said Ruby. "Why shouldn't I hear you? It's being unable to see you that bothers me. I can't tell much from a mirror. For instance, it looks like you're wearing these weird clothes. And I mean really weird: all the colors of the rainbow. Do you suppose this mirror works like a prism?"

Jeremiah looked down at the outfit he had put on that morning. It was a typical outfit for the children in Pineapple Place. Each of them owned some conventional clothes, of course, like the plaid shirt he had torn the day before. But generally they wore what April's mother knitted from lengths of yarn that Mrs. Pettylittle found in the trash. The yarn never matched, so Jeremiah could understand that the result was startling to a girl like Ruby. No one else at Athens Elementary was wearing sweat pants and a top knitted from purple, brown, and aqua wool. To make things worse, the cuff of his left pant leg was shocking pink. He drew that leg back and hid it behind the other.

"Why were you crying?" he asked, to change the subject.

"None of your business. Where did you come from, and why can't I see you except in mirrors? Why did you do my math problem? You don't look old enough to do sixth-grade fractions. You look more like a fourth grader to me. Why did you—"

"For your information," Jeremiah interrupted her, "I'm fifty-nine."

Ruby started to laugh and then frowned instead. "For your information, I'm not stupid. How old are you really? Why are you dressed like that? Are there more of you floating around? And what's your name if it isn't Jay? You don't have to answer if you don't want, but at least don't lie to me."

Jeremiah thought for a moment. He liked the sound

of Jay: it was neither sweet nor whiny, and it suited the new way he felt. "Go ahead and call me Jay," he said finally. "I'll tell you everything if you'll just stop asking questions and listen."

Another bell rang inside the school. Voices rose again, louder than before, and the whole building seemed to vibrate with the sound of chairs pushed back and scraping on the floor.

"That's for recess," Ruby said hurriedly. "Let's get out of here. I don't know about you, but I've had enough school for today."

9

They held hands. It was the only way to get ahead quickly, because when Ruby watched Jeremiah in her mirror, she kept bumping into parked cars and telephone poles, but when she didn't, she bumped into Jeremiah.

"This way," she urged him breathlessly. "Walk faster, can't you? Let's hope no one notices me leaving school early. Let's hope no one hears me talking, either, because I don't think other people can hear *you*. Ms. McAllister didn't hear you laugh, back in the girls' room. What were you doing in the girls' room, Jay? And listen, isn't there some way we can get rid of these dogs?"

Jeremiah looked behind him and counted eleven dogs. He chose to ignore them. "You ask too many questions."

Then he laughed. Hadn't he been aching for a friend in the outside world? Hadn't he been storing up questions he would ask if he ever found one? So Ruby had the right to ask him questions, too.

"I told you I'd explain everything," he said. "I wish we could go someplace quiet, though. I can't concentrate in the street."

"We're going to my place," Ruby said.

She crossed the last street, jaywalking just as she had the day before, and paused in front of the pharmacy. Jeremiah thought at first that she wanted to see if her uncle was inside, but realized she was staring at the pea-green remedy for cough.

"Uncle Homer is a fool," Ruby said crossly. "If only he kept his hobbies to himself, we wouldn't be in this fix. Last week's display was even worse: an infusion of pine-flower pollen as a cure for self-reproach. Did you see it?"

"I wasn't here last week," Jeremiah told her.

"Why not? Come on, let's get some lunch and you can tell me all about it." Ruby opened the door next to the pharmacy and led Jeremiah up a steep flight of stairs.

Until now, Jeremiah had felt uncomfortable in Athens, Connecticut. Its clean streets and quaint little shops bored him to tears. The townspeople, with their expensively casual clothes and their moon-faced blond children, seemed to have eggnog running through their veins instead of blood. He suspected that inside their houses, everything matched. But as soon as he walked into Homer Kourides' apartment, he felt at home. Like the houses in Pineapple Place, it looked as if it had been furnished slowly over the years. Like the houses in Pineapple Place, nothing matched. Unlike his own house, however, it was a mess.

"You may not believe this," Jeremiah told Ruby, "but it took me half a century before I really appreciated a mess like this."

Ruby shrugged out of her jacket and let it fall to the floor. She kicked off her sneakers. "That's a compliment?"

"It's a compliment." Jeremiah picked up Ruby's jacket and hung it with his own on a coatrack near the door. He had trouble finding room, because the rack was overloaded with coats and jackets, most of them worn or torn or missing buttons.

"Who lives here, anyway?" he asked.

"Just me and Uncle Homer," Ruby said. "You don't have to hang up my jacket, you know. It's already wrinkled."

She smiled at him in an old-fashioned oval mirror on the wall. The mirror was framed with ceramic roses whose pink petals were shaded by a thin gray film of dust. The mirror itself was so old that it was mottled with dark patches where the silver backing had worn away.

Jeremiah smiled in return. His smile widened as he caught sight of himself in his multicolored sweat suit. "I guess you think I look like a clown."

"That's all right," said Ruby. "Uncle Homer and

I don't care how people dress. It's just the rest of this town that does."

"I've got some normal clothes," said Jeremiah. "The thing is, they're hard to come by, so I keep them for special occasions, like birthday parties and moving days. Even so, they get worn out. We've had eight hundred birthday parties since we moved from Baltimore, fifty Christmases and Thanksgivings and that kind of day, and we've moved twenty-nine times."

Ruby gazed thoughtfully at his reflection in the rose-wreathed mirror. "Who is 'we'?" she asked.

Standing in the dim entrance to Homer Kourides' apartment, Jeremiah told her about Pineapple Place. He began with a description of their lives back in 1939 when the street, its six brick houses, and the families who lived in them were still in Baltimore.

"Mr. O'Malley owned a garage," he told Ruby. "My mother says he was too disorganized to make a profit from it, though. Mr. Todd worked in a bank, and Mr. Anderson was a doctor. My mother didn't do much of anything; she was a widow, and she was raising me. Mrs. Pettylittle was a widow, too, only she had a job in a department store, and then there were the Sweenys. Nobody knew what Mr. Sweeny did. We still don't. Except he had a million dollars, and that's come in handy over the past fifty years. Not that he doesn't owe us every penny of it, my mother says. After what he did to us."

"What did he do to you?" Ruby asked. "You can tell me while we're getting something to eat."

She led the way to a kitchen so small that when she opened the refrigerator door, Jeremiah had to back into the hall again.

"Pickled eggs?" asked Ruby. "Liverwurst?"

"I brought a sandwich," Jeremiah said. "I'll share."

Ruby cut Mr. Todd's bacon sandwich in two and put each half on a plate. She scooped two pickled eggs from a jar and cut a slab of liverwurst. "It's not very appetizing, is it?" she said.

"Not very," Jeremiah agreed.

"Well, we don't have to eat it. Uncle Homer doesn't expect me home for lunch on school days, you see, so he doesn't buy things like peanut butter and jelly. Let's see, do you want buttermilk or prune juice?"

"I brought some lemonade," Jeremiah said, secretly thankful, and he went back to the coatrack for the mason jar.

They sat in the living room, spreading dish towels on their laps. Ruby chose a high-backed chair that had been upholstered in prickly red plush. A cloud of dust rose into the air when she sat down, and Jeremiah thought he saw a moth. For himself, he picked a corner of a sofa that looked more cozy. It turned out to be too cozy: he sank through layers of feather cushions until his bottom hit the floor.

"Better move to the other end," Ruby advised. "The springs are broken where you are now. And don't worry about the lemonade: one more stain won't make any difference. Just go on with your story."

Jeremiah struggled free of the sofa and moved to another high-backed chair.

"There isn't that much left to tell. The war broke out in Europe, and Mr. Sweeny was an isolationist. He said America shouldn't get involved but if it did, Baltimore wasn't a safe place to be. So he isolated us. He moved Pineapple Place out of time, and we've been traveling around the world ever since. My mother says we should be grateful, but I heard her tell April's mother he should have asked us first."

Ruby took a bite of pickled egg and spat it out on the plate again. "You're a terrible storyteller," she said. "First you tell me all this ordinary stuff about Baltimore, and you go on and on. Then you say how Mr. Sweeny took you out of time and your whole street has been cruising around the world for fifty years, and I take it none of you gets any older either, do you? And all that part you stick in two sentences."

"That part is boring," said Jeremiah. "No matter how much I travel around, I'm still a prisoner in Pineapple Place. Don't you understand?"

"No," said Ruby, "but it sounds as if you and I could trade places and we'd both be a lot happier."

Jeremiah stuffed the last crusts of the bacon sandwich into his mouth and washed them down with the last drops of lemonade. "I don't think much of your town," he mumbled, "but I like your school. I could go to it if I lived here. Not just sixth grade, but seventh, and eighth, and ninth. A new grade every year. I'd like that. I'd like growing, too. Can you believe I've completely forgotten what it feels like to grow?''

"You don't feel it," Ruby informed him. "All you feel is the ends of your shoes, after it happens.''

"I'd like that," Jeremiah repeated, wiping his mouth on his sleeve and his sleeve on his pant leg. "We don't outgrow things in Pineapple Place. We just wear them out. And I'd like having you for a friend—except, if we traded places, Mr. Sweeny would move you away after a while.''

Ruby stood up and brushed the crumbs from her lap. She put Jeremiah's plate on top of her own and picked up the empty glasses. "I'm moving away anyway," she said over her shoulder as she walked toward the kitchen. "I'll be in California with a family I've never even met, just because this damn town with its damn elementary school thinks Uncle Homer is too old and crazy to take care of me anymore.''

A dim, brown shape shuffled into the room from the hallway. "I won't have swearing, Ruby. I'll assume that you said 'dumb' and let it go this time.''

"I said 'damn,' " said Ruby.

She let the plates and glasses fall with a splintering crash to the kitchen floor and threw her arms around Homer Kourides.

The Third Day

10

On Wednesday it rained. Rain darkened the sky, deadened the October leaves, made murky puddles among the cobblestones of Pineapple Place. A forsythia bush that grew outside the schoolroom window whipped long branches against the glass panes as the storm wind rose and fell. Mrs. Jenkins turned on all the lights.

"I hate New England," Jeremiah grumbled. "It's cold and dark, and it's going to get colder and darker all winter long. If we were in Greece, it would be different: stark, white limestone bluffs, dusty green olive orchards, and the clear, blue sea."

His mother sighed. "We're not in Greece, and I do wish you'd stop quoting that textbook. This is a charming little town, and we should make the best of it."

"It may be charming, but the rag-bagging is terrible," said April Anderson. "We've hardly found a thing since we came here, even at the dump. Mrs. Pettylittle says if the trash-flow problem isn't over soon, we'll be in real trouble.''

"I found a perfectly good umbrella this morning, outside a store,'' Jessie O'Malley announced smugly.

"You *stole* a perfectly good umbrella,'' said Mike. "Someone left it there while they were shopping.''

"Finders keepers,'' his sister chanted. She stuck out her tongue.

"We don't steal,'' Mike told her severely. "Next time we go out, I'm going to make you put it back.''

Jeremiah slipped his feet out of his shoes and tucked them under him in an effort to keep warm. "Mr. Sweeny brought us here by mistake,'' he said. "I keep telling you, but you won't listen. Mrs. Sweeny said he could call it a miscalculation, but it was really a mistake.''

April Anderson pursed her lips and raised her eyebrows. Tessie, Bessie, Jessie, Meggie, and Mike all exchanged meaningful glances.

"When did Mrs. Sweeny say that?'' April asked. "Were you there?''

"Sort of,'' said Jeremiah.

"Sort of a sneak,'' said Mike O'Malley. "Sort of spying again.''

Mrs. Jenkins intervened hastily. "Sit up straight, Jeremiah, and put your feet back on the floor. Good posture is the first step toward a good education. I don't know what you were up to yesterday, and if it was eavesdropping, I don't want to know. Instead of telling tales, you should be counting your blessings. At least we have food and shelter, and we're all in perfect health.''

Jeremiah sighed. He stretched his legs out stiffly and wiggled his feet back into his shoes. Opening a textbook whose yellowed pages were worn with fifty years of use, he studied two sentences that he had known by heart for as long as he could remember: "The Greek ships were stoutly built, which made them slower than Phoenician galleys. Driven by over a hundred oars, they would make an awesome sight even by present-day standards.''

"By 'present-day,' " he asked, "do they mean 1989, 1939, or 1911?''

His mother looked over his shoulder at the text. "Why 1911?''

"Because that's the copyright date on the first page of this book.''

Mrs. Jenkins reached down and flipped several pages. "That's not the part you're meant to be studying anyway. Here you go—'The Dark Ages and the Greek Renaissance.' ''

"Thanes, thralls, and churls," Jeremiah murmured dreamily.

Every head in the schoolroom jerked to attention. "What?'' said Mrs. Jenkins. "What kind of nonsense is that?''

"It isn't nonsense," said Jeremiah. "It's the Dark Ages. Thanes, thralls, and churls. They had repulsive pustules under their armpits and between their legs, and their breath smelled foul.''

A gleeful sound rose from the O'Malleys, and April's eyes twinkled.

Mrs. Jenkins walked over to the window and stared out at the rain. ''I don't know what's gotten into you,'' she said. ''Tearing your clothes, answering back, disappearing for hours on end—you used to be so docile, Jeremiah. Why this sudden change?''

In spite of the chill in the air, Jeremiah felt a delicious warmth spread through him. '' 'Change,' '' he repeated triumphantly. ''You said 'change'!''

''Well, that's only a manner of speaking, because of course in Pineapple Place we can't actually—''

Mrs. Jenkins stopped in the middle of her sentence to gasp. ''Mercy!''

Chairs scraped back as the children rushed to look out the window. Slowly picking his way across the wet cobblestones, hardly recognizable in an immense black oilcloth coat, came Mr. Sweeny. With one hand he grasped his silver-handled cane. With the other, he kept a firm grip on Mrs. Sweeny's arm. They were heading for the Jenkins house.

''But he never comes out. Never!'' Mrs. Jenkins said in an awed whisper. ''Only on celebration days and even then, not in the rain. Back to your seats, children, and let's give him a proper welcome.''

By the time the Sweenys had reached the front step and were knocking on the door, all seven children were at their desks smiling from ear to ear, except for Jeremiah, who wasn't in the mood for smiling. "Good morning, Mr. Sweeny, sir!" they chorused as he entered the schoolroom.

Mr. Sweeny grunted and lowered himself into the teacher's chair.

"Make yourself comfortable," Mrs. Jenkins said, hurrying to her parlor to fetch him a cushion. "Would you like to listen to our lessons? Can I make you a cup of tea?"

"No time," Mr. Sweeny snapped. "I'll come directly to the point: there has been gossip."

"Gossip?" Mrs. Jenkins echoed weakly. She looked around the room from child to child, letting her eyes rest slightly longer on her own son than the others.

Mr. Sweeny nodded several times. "Malicious gossip. Rumors of unrest. Undercurrents of dissent. Discordia. A fractious faction, a contumacious contingent. In other words—"

Jeremiah leaned forward eagerly. How could there possibly be other words?

As if he had heard the thought, Mr. Sweeny turned to fix him with a beady glare. "In other words, someone has been bellyaching, and I suspect it's you."

The other children laughed nervously and darted curious looks at Jeremiah as his mother came to his defense.

"Jeremiah is a good boy," she stated flatly. "Never a moment of trouble over all these years. There must be some mistake."

Mr. Sweeny frowned until his eyebrows met in the

middle. "I never make mistakes," he said in the same tones Jeremiah had heard from the cedar tree. "I don't miscalculate either, no matter what some fools may say."

Mrs. Sweeny turned pink in the face and made a twittering noise.

Mr. Sweeny coughed, spat into his pocket handkerchief, and handed the handkerchief to his wife, who folded it neatly and tucked it into her purse. Jeremiah thought it was a disgusting thing to do. He felt sorry for Mrs. Sweeny.

"If there's trouble, which I won't tolerate for one moment, it's all your fault!" Mr. Sweeny roared, looking from face to face in the schoolroom. "Bunch of fools! Where would you be if I hadn't saved you back in '39? Dead, that's where. Deceased, demised, defunct, deported, food for worms."

"Mercy, not the children!" his wife protested. "Even the twins would be only sixty-two, and that's still the prime of life."

She patted her gray curls and smiled at Bessie and Tessie.

"Dead," Mr. Sweeny repeated firmly. "Victims of the war."

Mrs. Sweeny's face turned pale again in her alarm. "Surely not, dear," she protested. "Because the Germans never bombed us after all, did they? Only Pearl Harbor, and although I couldn't tell you precisely where Pearl Harbor is, I believe it's quite some distance from Baltimore. And in any case, they weren't Germans, they were Japanese. Not that it would matter once the bombs had dropped, of course, but since they never dropped on Baltimore—''

"Dead!" Mr. Sweeny shouted, even louder than before. "You owe me your lives, every last one of you, and if I hear any more complaints about this paradise— this Eden—this jewel in the crown of the Eastern Sea-board—I'll move Pineapple Place to the South Pole. No, the North Pole: why should I give you the pleasure of penguins?"

His last words came out in a wheeze, and he coughed again. "Mark my words," he finished weakly. "I'm suffering from chronic cyclical anticipatory motion dis-comfort, which, as you may remember, precedes an-other move."

There was silence in the schoolroom. Mr. Sweeny was often crotchety, but there was usually a twinkle in his eye. Today there was no twinkle. Had the chilly New England weather put him in this mood? The chill sharpened as Jeremiah imagined autumn in the North Pole: it would be much worse. Timidly, he raised his hand.

"Yes?" Mr. Sweeny folded his arms and glowered at him in an uncompromising way.

"What can we do, sir? To stay where we are, I mean, instead of moving to the North Pole?"

"Why?" Mr. Sweeny demanded. "Why should you care to stay? You were the source of the disturbance, were you not? Admit it."

Jeremiah looked at the other children's faces. They clearly expected him to deny it or put the blame on someone else. It made him so mad that he forgot to be afraid. "Yes," he said. "I was, but I changed my mind."

Mr. Sweeny struggled to his feet with the help of his wife and his silver-handled cane. "The fact that you changed your mind doesn't mean that I'll change mine. If you want to get back in my good graces, solve the trash-flow problem. This is our third day here, isn't it? Well, I'll give you just three more days."

"Thank you," Jeremiah whispered, and the other children echoed, "Thank you, Mr. Sweeny, sir."

Mr. Sweeny shook his cane at them. "Any more trouble and you'll have only yourselves to thank!"

11

Jeremiah ran along the slick sidewalks of the town until he reached Flo's Acropolis Diner. He would have run all the way to the pharmacy, but was forced to stop because of a stitch in his side. The pencil he had jammed into his sweat pants pocket had poked a hole through the cloth and was scratching his thigh. He pulled it out and scrawled a message in his copybook:

I NEED HELP!

That ought to do for a start, and if Ruby was home from school, he wouldn't need it after all.

He hugged his arms to his chest, doubled over and breathed deeply, but remained in pain. Massaging his ribs didn't help either. He sat down, which was more comfortable but made him sleepy, too. He closed his eyes.

The next thing Jeremiah knew, he was sprawled on the sidewalk. The pain in his side had grown so bad that it overflowed into his head, but it was no longer due to running. Someone had tripped over him, striking him hard in the ribs with a rubber-booted foot. Scattered on the sidewalk was what had recently been souvlaki. Next to it, for all the world to see, was Jeremiah's note.

In spite of the pain, Jeremiah was already moving away when he saw that the man who had tripped over him was Ruby's uncle.

His heart sank. If there had been the slightest chance of persuading Homer Kourides to help him solve the trash-flow problem, it was ruined now. What should he do? Help the man to his feet and scrape what was left of the souvlaki into the paper bag, or give up and run away?

Before Jeremiah could decide, Homer Kourides reached out and grabbed the note. " 'I need help,' " he read aloud. He sat up, rubbed his knees and elbows, and read it again even louder: " 'I NEED HELP!' "

The door of the Acropolis Diner opened, and a woman in a white apron appeared. "Whadya do, Homer, take a spill?"

Ruby's uncle folded the note and slipped it into his pocket. "Looks like it," he said. "I'm okay, Flo. Nothing broken, that's all that matters."

"You gotta watch it," Flo warned. "Wait there, I'll be right back."

She was gone for two or three minutes, time enough for Ruby's uncle to stand up and peel off the wet autumn leaves that were pasted against his clothes. When she returned, she held a second paper bag.

"The reason I say you gotta watch it," she continued, "is you know how they are in this town. They'll say you've been hitting the bottle, and you got troubles enough without that, don't you?"

"She's right," Homer Kourides said after Flo had gone back into the diner. "Better not try that one again, Jay Jenkins. Why didn't you just come knock on my door?"

"That's where I was headed for," Jeremiah explained. "How was I supposed to know—"

He stopped when he realized that Ruby's uncle couldn't hear a word. "Oh, forget it."

He reached into his pocket, but the pencil was no longer there. It wouldn't have been much use anyway, because Ruby's uncle had grabbed him by the elbow and was hustling him along the street at a speed that hardly left him time to breathe.

"Good thing Ruby warned me about you," he muttered, pinching Jeremiah's elbow so hard that it ached. "Could have made a fool of myself, otherwise. And Flo was right: I can't afford that. Do you know Flo?"

Jeremiah shook his head, although he knew Ruby's uncle couldn't see him do it.

"She has a heart of gold. Smell that!" Homer Kourides, in an attempt to bring the paper bag closer to Jeremiah's nose, smacked him in the face with it. "My apologies," he said. "Sincere apologies, although I can't think of anything I'd rather be hit with than souvlaki. I'll give you a taste when we get back home. Just so we leave some for Ruby."

When they reached the pharmacy, Homer Kourides held the door open and carefully tested the space around him to be sure Jeremiah wasn't in the way before shutting it again.

Unfortunately, the pharmacy was full of customers. A woman with a stroller was pricing disposable diapers in one aisle, and two others were trying on sunglasses in the next. A bunch of teenagers stood in front of the magazine rack. Over by the cash register, a woman was waiting impatiently, tapping the counter with her fingernails and shifting her weight from one foot to another. It was Ms. McAllister.

Homer Kourides hurried up to her. "Are you ready to make your purchase?" he gasped, dropping the second bag of souvlaki on the counter, where it sprang open and let out a waft of fragrant steam.

"Where were you?" Ms. McAllister asked in an exasperated voice. "How can you leave your shop unattended?"

Jeremiah knocked a can of talcum powder to the floor as he edged past the stroller, moving to a spot where he could hear Ruby's teacher more clearly.

"I have to be back in class in seven minutes," Ms. McAllister said. "I came because you promised to let me know about Ruby's departure plans, but I haven't heard from you."

Ruby's uncle wrung his hands in a gesture that had become familiar to Jeremiah. "To tell the truth, we haven't set a date."

"Why not? Ruby's behavior has been disturbing in the past few days, to say the least. All this uncertainty is bad for the child. Surely you understand."

Ruby's uncle sighed. He spread out his fingers and stared at the pale, blue-veined knuckles. "Ruby wants to stay."

Ms. McAllister screwed up her forehead and fixed him with pleading eyes. Jeremiah realized they were friendly eyes. It looked as if she cared about Ruby. But if she cared, why couldn't she see that Ruby was happy with her uncle?

"We've already discussed this," she said, reasoning gently with Homer Kourides as if he were a child himself. "You promised to settle on a date with the family out in California, and you promised to call the airline. There's no cause for further delay. I have to get back to my students, but I expect to hear from you, Mr. Kourides. Remember, now!"

After she left, the teenagers bought one magazine, the woman with the stroller paid for her Pampers, and the other women left without buying anything at all. Homer Kourides shut the door behind them, bolted it, and flipped over the sign that read YES, WE'RE OPEN! so that it read SORRY, WE'RE CLOSED.

"Good riddance!" he said. "Nuisances, all of them."

Jeremiah laughed.

"Ruby won't be home from school until after three," Homer Kourides continued. "She was hoping you'd be there to keep her company. Can you stay?"

Jeremiah knew it was useless to reply.

"No telling if you answer me or not. Never mind, I'll soon fix that." Homer Kourides went to the back of the shop, where a row of shelves reached from the floor up to the ceiling. A quarter of the shelf space was occupied by prescription drugs. The rest was crammed with jars and bottles containing twigs, dried leaves and flowers, and liquids like the one in the window display in colors varying from black to the palest lavender. He ran his hand lovingly along a row of bottles, selecting one with an orange liquid and one with blue. After setting them on the counter, he climbed a stepladder and handed down a dozen jars from the highest shelves.

"Do you care to know what you'll be swallowing?" he asked as he placed a mortar and pestle on the counter.

"I'm not sure," said Jeremiah.

"Still can't hear you. Never mind, I'll assume you do—unlike the pigheads in this town who willingly poison themselves and their innocent children as long as the product has been advertised on TV."

Jeremiah watched closely as a dribble of the blue liquid was measured into the mortar, followed by a dribble of the orange.

"My own concoctions," Homer Kourides said. "I won't tell you what's in them for fear of spoiling your appetite, but you can trust me."

He returned the bottles to their places on the shelf before continuing. "Here we go. This may interest you, if you know your herbs."

Dipping his fingers into one jar after another, he recited, "Mimulus for fear of the dark, and mustard for gloom. Wormwood for boredom, and honeysuckle for those who live too much in the past. Spanish chestnut for those who have reached the end of their tether— which is part of your problem, according to my niece— and catnip for the nerves. Water violet for those who are too proud to mingle with others, nettle for anemia, figwort for dandruff, dropwort for loss of hair, lungwort for loss of voice, and scurvy grass for the obese. Drink up!"

Jeremiah opened his mouth to protest. This was a mistake, because Homer Kourides aimed a ladle full of the mixture at his face, and a portion of it splashed inside his mouth.

"I am not obese," Jeremiah said after swallowing.

"So I see." Ruby's uncle dabbed at Jeremiah's clothes with a dusty rag. "How was I to know? It won't do you the slightest harm, by the way. It's not as it if would make you lose weight."

"If it doesn't make you lose weight, how does it help the obese?" Jeremiah asked crossly. The mixture had not only tasted horrid, it left an oily feeling in his mouth and a burning feeling in his throat.

"When they're eating scurvy grass they can't be eating something else," said Homer Kourides, "and scurvy grass has very few calories. That's obvious, isn't it? Use your brains."

"I don't have dandruff, either," Jeremiah grumbled, "and I haven't lost my hair or my voice, and I'm not anemic."

Homer Kourides put the lids back on the jars and the jars back on the shelves. He poured the remainder of his mixture into a bottle and slipped the bottle into his pocket. "It was the closest I could get to the symptoms of invisibility," he reasoned. "Why complain? It worked."

Jeremiah hurried to the cosmetics counter and gazed at himself in a mirror. He looked just the same as when he had been invisible. He ran his hands up and down his sides, but he felt the same, too. He stuck out his tongue: it was oily and slightly blue, but otherwise the same old tongue.

"Are you sure it worked?"

Homer Kourides led him to the front of the store where he could examine him in the light of day. "Of course I'm sure. You seem like a normal child to me, except for a slight eccentricity in your apparel. Everyone can see you, young man, so mind you keep out of mischief. Now if you'll excuse me, I think I have a customer."

Still holding Jeremiah's hand, he slid back the bolt, turned the key, and opened the pharmacy door. Right in front of them, breathless and a little flushed, stood Mrs. Pettylittle. She puffed, and panted, and patted her cheeks with her black-gloved hands.

"You said to return if I needed help," she told Homer Kourides. "So I did, although our trash-flow problem is getting so out of hand that I'm afraid help is an impossibility."

Homer Kourides beckoned her into the shop. "I'd be delighted to help you," he said. "Nothing is impossible for a man who has just invented a visibility potion."

Mrs. Pettylittle stared at Jeremiah. "Visibility potion? Do you mean this child is visible to the public? What can you be thinking of?"

A hurt expression flashed across Homer Kourides' face. "I thought you would be pleased!"

"Pleased? Don't you realize that he can no longer go home? I'm the only visible being that can go in and out of Pineapple Place. Change him back this instant!"

But Jeremiah had already slipped by her, into the street.

12

Visibility was a strange sensation. Jeremiah felt as if he stuck out like a sore thumb. Several people greeted him as they walked by under umbrellas, and a woman in a station wagon slowed down to stare at his multicolored clothes. They embarrassed him, and so did his lace-up leather shoes. For the first time in fifty years he felt self-conscious.

He also felt cold. The wind had died down and the rain had weakened to a drizzle, but he was wet to the bone and anxious to get home. His mother would fuss at him with towels and draw him a hot bath. She would make him cocoa with a marshmallow floating on top. With luck, she would be too upset to remember Mr. Sweeny's visit. Tired as he was, Jeremiah broke into a run.

Water trickled down from his rain-soaked curls,

stinging his eyes and blinding him, so it was no surprise when he missed the entrance to Pineapple Place. But when he turned and ran more slowly down the block again, he began to worry. Had Mrs. Pettylittle been right? He tried a third time, at a walk.

"It's got to be here," Jeremiah said aloud. "I know this was the spot."

"Lost-something?" a gruff voice asked behind him.

He turned and saw a patrol car parked along the curb. A police officer had rolled down the window of the driver's seat and was looking him over in a kindly but expectant way.

Jeremiah searched helplessly for signs of Pineapple Place. He knew he was on the right block: there was the gabled, green-shuttered house he had seen from the cedar tree the morning after they moved to Athens. There were the elm trees, the asphalt driveway, the basketball net over the garage door. But Pineapple Place was gone.

Jeremiah said the first thing that came into his head. "I lost my dog."

The police officer rolled the window farther down. "My name is Frank Rossotti. What's yours?"

Jeremiah knew that Officer Rossotti, like everyone else who could now see him, was staring at his clothes. "Jay Jenkins," he said. "I got caught in the rain. I think I'd better go home."

"Good idea. What breed of dog?"

Jeremiah shivered, and not just from the cold. "All

kinds," he said. Realizing that he had failed to convince the policeman, he added, "Mostly Chihuahua."

Officer Rossotti lifted his left eyebrow and pulled down the corners of his mouth.

Jeremiah panicked. "There he goes!" he yelled, pointing toward a clump of bushes, and he ran.

Where could he find shelter? He didn't want to go back to the pharmacy, and it was a long way to Ruby's school. Still, the school was the only place he could think of, and he needed to talk to Ruby.

By the time he reached the school grounds, the sun was out again and he felt a little warmer. This was a comfort until he noticed that his clothes had begun to steam. A strong smell of wet wool tickled his nostrils, and his skin began to itch. He abandoned the idea of going inside. Instead he sat down in the same corner of the playground where he had waited for Ruby the day before.

"Come home with me and I'll find you something else to wear," Ruby said when she finally joined him after school was out.

Jeremiah glanced down at his knit outfit and groaned. "I'm sorry. I know it's awful."

"It isn't awful when it's dry," said Ruby. "In fact, I kind of like it. Want to trade?"

Ruby was dressed in faded jeans and an old flannel shirt that was too big for her. Jeremiah suspected it had once belonged to her uncle. It looked comfortable, and he was overcome by the desire to wear it himself.

"Sure," he said. "Let's trade."

Ruby's eyes laughed at him through her pale-rimmed glasses. "If you people were visible, you'd have to watch out what you wear. In this town, if you're not exactly like everyone else they think you're crazy. They already think Uncle Homer and I are crazy. Want to know why we moved to this town in the first place?"

Jeremiah nodded.

"Same reason as you, only it wasn't a mistake. We moved here because we couldn't go to Greece."

"Why did you want to go to Greece?" Jeremiah asked.

"Why not? We had a better reason than you did, actually. My father and Uncle Homer were second-generation Americans. They were born in Brooklyn, but their parents came from Greece. And they were really terrific people—my grandparents, I mean—educated, and all that. Only their English wasn't good, so they ended up with these really crummy jobs. My grandfather worked as a night watchman, would you believe it? And my grandmother did housework for the kind of women who would be working for *her*, back in the old country."

"Your uncle is pretty smart," Jeremiah observed. "He really knows his stuff with those herbs and things, doesn't he!"

"Nature's Way?" Ruby made a disgusted face. "That's another story. But yes, he's smart enough. So was my father. His name was Sophocles."

Jeremiah let out a whoop of laughter and Ruby

looked hurt. "You're as bad as the people in this town: anything different has got to be funny. Sophocles is a perfectly good name. At least it shows respect for a great philosopher. A jay is just a bird."

To change the subject, Jeremiah told about Mr. Sweeny's promise. "It's like a bad joke, because there's a Parthenon and an Acropolis in this town, and your uncle's name is Homer. Now you say his brother's name was Sophocles. All I need is the Aegean Sea!"

Ruby didn't laugh. "They wanted to go back to Athens and be Greek. My father married a girl from California and she said she'd like to move to Athens, too, only they both died in a car accident when I was three years old."

"But you survived?"

"Do I look dead? I wasn't in the crash. I was home in bed, with Uncle Homer looking after me, and he kept on looking after me. My mother's family out in California said that was okay, but they wouldn't let him move to Greece. They said if he did, they'd sue for custody. So he moved to Athens, Connecticut, instead, kind of like a bad joke."

"Just for a joke?" Jeremiah was shocked. Mr. Sweeny had moved Pineapple Place twenty-nine times, each time for a different reason, but so far the reason had never been a joke.

"No," said Ruby. "He also moved here because it has one of the finest school systems in the country."

She started laughing. It was an unpleasant laugh: brittle, and a little shrill.

Jeremiah grabbed her arm and shook it. "Stop! That isn't funny. Tell me, if he didn't take you to Greece and he got you into such a good school system, how come your uncle can't keep you anymore?"

Ruby wiped her eyes on the back of her hand. "I told you: we're different. Uncle Homer is even more different than I am, and you have to admit I'm not like the other kids in this town. And I'm growing up—I'll be in junior high next year. So a bunch of busybodies like Ms. McAllister, and the guidance teacher, and a couple of social workers—they started saying how Uncle Homer wasn't a suitable person to bring up a teenage girl. They wrote to those relatives out in California and arranged for me to live with them."

"Is that legal?" Jeremiah asked.

Ruby gave him a scornful look. "Legal! Anything is legal if you're respectable enough. The people in this town are all respectable, and they think Uncle Homer isn't. What's more, he doesn't have a penny, because instead of selling people expensive prescription drugs he gives them Nature's Way, so he couldn't afford a lawyer if he went to court."

"You sound as if you hate this place," Jeremiah said.

Ruby shook her head impatiently. "Only the parts that keep me and Uncle Homer from being happy together. But some parts are nice. Like there's a swampy place on the shore, if you follow the street school is on all the way to the end. It's a place with rushes and rocks, and if you sit in the right spot no one can see you, even from the water. No one but me and Uncle Homer goes there. I'll take you there one day."

They walked for a while in silence. Jeremiah wanted to ask more questions, but he was afraid Ruby would start laughing the peculiar laugh again and never stop. He was trembling with anger for her. How could people move her away and set her down among strangers without asking her opinion? Of course, that was exactly what Mr. Sweeny had done twenty-nine times to the people in Pineapple Place, but at least they traveled together. Ruby would be alone.

Jeremiah stopped in his tracks. He was alone now, too! Pineapple Place was gone. Had Mr. Sweeny changed his mind and moved it to the North Pole without waiting three more days? Without even waiting for Jeremiah? Or was it still there, only he couldn't see it anymore because of Homer Kourides' concoction?

"Ruby, I'm in trouble, too—," he began. Suddenly he looked around and saw that she had taken him to a part of town where he had never been before. "Where are we? I thought we were going back to your place to trade clothes."

"My clothes wouldn't fit you," Ruby said. "Besides, this shirt belonged to my father, and I want to keep it. Don't worry, I have an idea."

They were in a shopping mall, the kind Jeremiah had often seen in New England. It looked like a row of colonial townhouses at first, but turned out to be modern. There was an A & P, a Radio Shack, a Woolworth's, and a gigantic drugstore that probably attracted all the customers who were suspicious of Nature's Way. Ruby wasn't taking him to a store, however. She headed for a large metal bin at the back of the parking lot. On the bin was written FRIENDLY NEIGHBORS, INC. DEPOSIT USED CLOTHING IN SLOT.

"See?" Ruby said triumphantly. "That's no slot—that's a window. You can climb right in and pick out something that really fits."

"But wouldn't that be stealing?" Jeremiah asked, remembering how shocked Mrs. Pettylittle had been when he had suggested it.

"Of course not," said Ruby. "It's charity. People put stuff here for the needy. You're needy, aren't you?"

It was too good to be true. Before he had even started to explain to Ruby about the trash-flow problem and Mr. Sweeny's ultimatum, she had led him straight to the answer.

"Are there bins for other things too?" Jeremiah asked excitedly. "Lag bolts, flatheads, and dowel screws? Rubber spatulas? Split-wing toggles?"

Ruby gaped at him. "Split-wing whats? Oh, don't just stand there talking. I'm hungry, and Uncle Homer said he'd get souvlaki. Go in and find some clothes so we can go home."

She gave Jeremiah a boost that sent him tumbling headfirst into the bin. It was like falling on a haystack, or a feather bed: he bounced, and sank into a soft heap of what felt like winter coats.

"Ruby, it's dark!" he said. The words echoed strangely in the bin.

"What did you say?" Ruby's voice was small, and thin, and far away.

"I can't see!" Jeremiah shouted. "It's dark in here!"

"Throw some stuff out and I'll look at it for you," Ruby suggested.

Groping around him, Jeremiah selected items that he hoped were shirts and trousers of the proper size. He lifted them over his head and pushed them out the slot to Ruby. Some of them were pushed right in again.

"That's a skirt, dummy!" Ruby shouted. "Hurry up, I'm starved."

Jeremiah groped around some more. "How's this?" he asked, tossing out another armful.

There was no answer.

"Ruby! Was that okay? Do we have enough?"

Still no answer. He hoisted himself to the level of the slot and peered out. Peering back at him with outraged disbelief was the police officer from the patrol car.

"Find your Chihuahua?" Frank Rossotti asked.

13

"Of course he's my boy," Mrs. Pettylittle stated firmly. "Mr. Kourides has already told you that. What I'd like to know is, what's he doing in a police station?"

"Good question," said Officer Rossotti. "Your name, please?"

"Pettylittle."

"First name?"

"Letty."

By what stroke of luck had she come to Jeremiah's rescue? He looked at her questioningly, but failed to catch her eye.

"And the boy?" Officer Rossotti continued. "What's the boy's name?"

"Surely he told you his name himself. It's Jeremiah."

"Jay is what he told me," Officer Rossotti said accusingly, "and Jenkins, not Pettylittle."

"Did I say otherwise?" Mrs. Pettylittle smoothed her tippet, tugged at her gloves, and smiled. "What's the trouble, Officer? We're new in town, and the boy doesn't know his way around. I'm afraid there's been some misunderstanding."

"He knows his way around the Friendly Neighbors bin," Officer Rossotti informed her. "Tossing out old clothes to Ruby here. I don't know what they wanted them for, but it amounts to petty theft."

Homer Kourides wrung his hands and turned to Ruby in bewilderment. "Old clothes, Ruby? May I ask—"

Ruby blinked rapidly behind her pale-rimmed glasses. "I'm sorry, Uncle Homer. We didn't think anyone would mind."

Officer Rossotti looked Mrs. Pettylittle up and down in a deliberating way. "This isn't the first time we've met, is it, ma'am? May I ask where you are staying?"

Jeremiah couldn't help but admire her. She was in a fix, but no one would guess it from her face. It remained respectably blank as she searched for a plausible answer.

Homer Kourides came to the rescue. "She's staying with us."

Mrs. Pettylittle was quick to agree. "Just a short visit, of course. Homer and I are old friends, and it's nice to get the children together, isn't it, Officer?"

"So long as they stay out of trouble," he answered. "You never know what kids will get into next. Grown-ups either, for that matter. Saw you the other morning, didn't I, ma'am? Out—walking?"

"Quite likely. I was getting to know your town. It seems unusually clean."

"We hope it stays that way," said Officer Rossotti as he led them to the door.

Mrs. Pettylittle wore her smile for several blocks after leaving the police station. Then she lost it, along with her temper.

"Meddlesome, that's the only word for it," she snapped. "Why you had to interfere I'll never understand. Who asked you to make the child visible? If you wanted to talk to him, you could have done it through me and avoided all this trouble. Now, you're to go straight home and give him some medicine that will bring him back to normal. Biotics, or antibiotics—I don't care what, as long as they work."

Homer Kourides rubbed his chin thoughtfully while he shuffled along beside her. "It goes against the grain to use prescription drugs when a child can be cured by Nature's Way."

"Use Nature's Way then. Use it fast."

Homer Kourides shook his head. "Won't work."

"Won't work? Won't work!" Mrs. Pettylittle's voice rose shrilly. "Do you mean to say he'll have this handicap forever?"

"Heavens no, not forever," Ruby's uncle said. "The effect ought to wear off after four to six hours, according to my calculations. I dosed him about three hours ago. All we can do now is wait.''

They waited. Ruby put on the kettle to make herb tea. Homer Kourides reheated the souvlaki and served it as a late lunch, with baklava for dessert. By the time Jeremiah was licking the honey from his fingers, he had begun to fade. To his disappointment, he looked the same in the mirror.

"Visible, invisible, or half-and-half, it doesn't seem to make much difference," he complained.

"How do you feel?" Ruby asked.

"Exactly the same, no matter what. Except for when your uncle sloshed his potion in my mouth. Then I felt sick. What do I look like when I'm half-and-half?''

"As if I were seeing a tree through a snowstorm," Ruby said. "I can see lights through you. I could read a book through you.'' She looked depressed, and poked at her baklava with a fork. She had hardly touched it or the souvlaki.

When Mrs. Pettylittle and Ruby's uncle had finished eating, they went through all the cupboards in search of things for Pineapple Place. They found a jar of nuts and bolts for Mr. Todd, and a rubber spatula for Jeremiah's mother. Ruby's uncle dropped a pile of magazines into an old army duffel bag and stuffed some plastic bread bags on top. He produced old calendars from every year since 1978. He added some flowerpots, two lampshades, and a new purple bathmat.

"Never liked purple," he explained when Mrs.

Pettylittle said it was too good to accept. "You'll be doing me a favor. And keep the duffel bag, by the way. Never could stand the army, either."

He went to a closet and returned with a hot-water bottle, some wire hangers, and a pair of bedroom slippers. Mrs. Pettylittle bounced after him, chirping with delight. Between chirps she entertained him with the history of Pineapple Place, starting with its first move from Baltimore to Phoenix, Arizona, in 1939, and going on from there.

Meanwhile, Ruby grew more and more depressed. "I can't see you at all anymore," she announced at last.

"I guess that means I can go home," said Jeremiah.

"Will you be coming back?"

"Of course," he said. "Now that we have all the stuff your uncle gave us, Mr. Sweeny won't move us to the North Pole. You'll probably be gone before we are."

Ruby's mouth trembled, and her glasses fogged up as tears swam in her eyes. "It's too bad I can't see you, at least for the rest of the time I'm here. It's no fun talking to reflections."

Jeremiah agreed. "I wish I could swallow a mirror or something, and reflect myself automatically."

Ruby looked thoughtful. "Uncle Homer!" she called to the next room, where her uncle was sorting through old socks. "Do you have any herbs that would make a person reflect?"

There was a long silence before Homer Kourides

answered. "That's tricky, my dear. There's rosemary for remembrance, of course, and olive blossoms for mental fatigue. Purslane, and pokeweed, and amaranth are all beneficial to the functions of the brain, but reflection—well, I couldn't say. In India, the lotus is linked with spiritual thought. I don't believe they eat it, though. If a customer came to me for advice, chances are I would recommend garlic."

Ruby brightened up. "Why garlic, Uncle Homer?"

"Why not?" he replied. "It's known for its medicinal powers, its magical powers—keeps off evil spirits, all that nonsense. And in the presence of garlic, a person always thinks twice. Now, if that's not reflection, I'd like to know what is."

His normally quiet voice curled into peals of laughter as he slammed the sock drawer shut and opened one containing underwear.

The hopeful look left Ruby's face. "That's not funny. You know perfectly well what kind of reflection I mean."

"I'm sorry," he said. "I wish I could help you, but nothing comes to mind at present."

Mrs. Pettylittle buttoned the jet-black buttons on her scarlet coat. She went to the mirror, dabbed at her nose with a lace handkerchief, and fluffed out her veil. "You've already done more than we deserve," she said. "I don't know how to thank you enough—isn't there something I can do for you?"

Ruby shook her head sadly, but Homer Kourides

got a most peculiar look on his face: a look that Jeremiah would have described as half happy, half sad. "I don't suppose——," he began. He cleared his throat, scratched the back of his neck, ruffled up his hair, and smiled his tilted smile. "I don't suppose you would marry me?"

Mrs. Pettylittle froze just as she was, with one hand lifted to her veil and the other clutching her lace handkerchief. The only sign of life was the slow blush that spread across her face.

The Fourth Day

14

"Why shouldn't she?" Jeremiah asked his mother. "Give me one good reason."

"Give me one good reason why she should."

"Because it would make three people happy," Jeremiah argued. "If Mr. Kourides had a wife, Ruby wouldn't have to go to California. She'd be part of a real family."

"What difference will that make to you when we're in the North Pole?" Mrs. Jenkins shivered. "This will be our worst move yet, and it's all your fault. How could you do such a thing to your mother?"

"Don't worry, it's not going to happen," said Jeremiah. "I'm solving the trash-flow problem, aren't I?"

"Don't get your hopes up. And keep your fingers out of the batter, there's a good boy."

Mrs. Jenkins stirred vigorously with a wooden spoon. Then she picked up her new rubber spatula and scraped the batter into a baking pan.

"There's nothing left to lick!" Jeremiah complained.

"Of course not," said his mother. "That's the whole point of a rubber spatula: no waste. Now tell me, have you considered poor Mrs. Pettylittle in this scheme of yours? She's been comfortably widowed for the best part of a century. Why should she want to marry again?"

"Because Mr. Kourides is a nice man, and Ruby is wonderful."

"She wouldn't be marrying Ruby, whoever that may be. Besides, why on earth would she want to spend an eternity in Athens, Connecticut?"

While his mother turned away to check the oven temperature, Jeremiah plunged his finger into the pan of cake batter and transferred it quickly to his mouth. "I wish *I* could," he said after swallowing. "Not an eternity, but at least until I finish high school."

Mrs. Jenkins slid the cake pan carefully onto the middle rack, shut the oven door, and set the timer. She ran her hands under the tap and wiped off the kitchen counter. Jeremiah could tell from the way she wrung out the dishrag that she was cross. He glanced out the window, thinking he might be wise to go for a walk. Then he decided to have it out with her. "What's wrong?"

His mother gave the rag a final vicious wring that

produced three drops of water. "Why should anything be wrong?"

"You're mad about something. I can tell."

Mrs. Jenkins sighed and let her arms hang limply. "Your father tended to be self-centered, too. It must be inherited. May I ask what makes high school so important that for your sake sixteen people should settle permanently in this town?"

"Not permanently. Just until—"

"I heard you. But even supposing you went up a grade each year, you'd still have eight more years before you graduated from high school. Pineapple Place has never stayed over two years in one spot, that I can remember."

Jeremiah knew from experience that no matter what he said or did, his mother would treat him like a baby. He knew he ought to know better than to go on trying, but he gave her one last chance. "Actually, it would only be six more years. I tried sixth grade with Ruby, and I could do the work just fine. It was Middle Ages, not American history, but that was fun. And the math was really easy."

Mrs. Jenkins let her breath out in one long puff and sat down quickly on a kitchen chair. "Sixth grade? What do you mean? Who is this Ruby?"

Jeremiah told her. He started with Columbus Day Observed and went on to his first day at school. He described Ruby, and Ruby's uncle. Although he mentioned Nature's Way, he didn't say he had swallowed some of it and become visible. He doubted his mother would be happy to learn about his visit to the Athens police station.

As he talked, his mother grew increasingly pale. "Are you trying to tell me you've been seen?"

"Well, mostly in mirrors. It was no big deal."

"No big deal?" Mrs. Jenkins passed her hand lightly across her face, as if to make sure it was still there. "But this is terrible, Jeremiah! You, of all people—I can't believe it."

"It's true. Ask Mrs. Pettylittle."

"She knows? Then the whole street will know. I'll never live this down."

Jeremiah shuffled his feet impatiently. "Why should they care? All of the other kids have been seen and nothing bad happened. So why act as if I'd killed somebody?"

"It's killing me." His mother sighed dramatically, but the sigh broke off as her attention was caught by the rubber spatula still lying on the table. "Where did that come from? I take it you didn't find it in the trash after all. That would be too good to be true."

"Mr. Kourides gave it to me. I told him you wanted one, and he said to take it because he had more kitchen stuff than he knew what to do with."

A slight teariness in Mrs. Jenkins's eyes brightened into a gleam. "Gave it to you? Just like that?"

"He was glad to get rid of it," Jeremiah explained. "He had two of them. His kitchen is so full of stuff, I bet he has two of everything."

"What, for instance?"

"Oh, the usual."

She sighed again. "How can you talk about *usual* when you know how little we have? Even the sturdiest utensils wear out over half a century, and rag-bagging has been no help at all."

"Well, now you have your rubber spatula, so you ought to be grateful instead of nagging at me."

Mrs. Jenkins made a quick gesture, swatting at gratitude as if it were a fly. "It may be unchristian of me, but it rankles when people have too much and we have so little. Does he have two blenders?"

"What's a blender?"

"Oh, don't be foolish, Jeremiah. You know perfectly well: the Andersons have one. Just think of the time I'd save if I didn't have to beat the batter three hundred strokes with a spoon."

Jeremiah thought. If anything seemed foolish, it was counting strokes when you had all the time in the world. In his opinion, one of the few advantages of living forever was that you could take your time.

"I didn't notice any blenders," he told his mother. "How did we get started on blenders? We were talking about school."

"School is out of the question," his mother said. "You couldn't afford it, for one thing. You'd have to buy supplies: textbooks, and notebooks, and pencils, and all that."

Jeremiah thought for a moment. "I don't think so. This is public school, so you get those things for free."

His mother wiped her eyes and smiled dreamily. "Free? Even for us?"

"Even for us," said Jeremiah. "This is the United States of America! Remember what you taught us? 'One nation invisible, with liberty and justice for all.' "

"That's not quite how it goes," his mother said.

"It's what you taught us," Jeremiah insisted. "Besides, there are special laws now for handicapped children, and isn't invisibility a handicap? So we have as much right to supplies as normal kids."

His voice quavered as he finished this speech. He wasn't as sure of himself as he pretended, and he was afraid his mother would be angry.

Instead, she looked as if Christmas had come and she had gotten everything she wanted. "Do you think you could bring home some textbooks and a supply of paper? It bothers me to see you children doing your sums on smoothed-out paper bags. And lots of new, long pencils. I'm sick and tired of two-inch, tooth-marked stubs with the erasers bitten off."

Jeremiah laughed nervously. "Bring them home? Where from?"

"From school, of course." Mrs. Jenkins clapped her hands. "Your father would be proud of you: our little family provider! I can't wait until Mrs. O'Malley hears about it. She'll be green with envy."

Jeremiah wondered how many times his mother had described Mrs. O'Malley as "green with envy." Didn't she know that, on the contrary, Mrs. O'Malley pitied her for having such a namby-pamby son? He had tried to change in the last few days, but if anyone heard him described as "our little family provider," his hard work would amount to nothing.

"You still haven't told me how I can get all that stuff," he said. "It's not as if I could just walk into the school and ask. They can't see me or hear me, and they wouldn't give it to me if they could."

"They have a supply room, don't they?" his mother asked. "You can easily find out where it is. I'll give you a nice bag to put it all in, and you can go back again if it's too heavy."

For the first time in his life, Jeremiah was shocked at his mother. "I didn't mean I could go and cart away whole bags of stuff. The school might give me a couple of textbooks, only I'd have to give them back at the end of the year. But not stacks of textbooks, and paper, and new pencils. That's just plain stealing."

It was obvious that his mother hadn't heard a word of his last statement. She gazed at him with pride in her expression. "My little man!"

Jeremiah shuddered. "I'll see if I can get some things. Some, not a lot. But don't tell anyone, especially the O'Malleys."

"You always were too modest," his mother said fondly. "I'll pack you a nice picnic lunch. And oh, Jeremiah, do ask Ruby's uncle if he has two blenders!"

15

Jeremiah got to school early and hid in the boys' room until the last of the dogs lost his scent and trotted away. He couldn't risk being found by anyone, not even Ruby. After the bell had rung and the children were settled at their desks, he would scout around for a supply room. Until then, he would play it safe.

He didn't like the boys' room. The floral-scented deodorizer didn't mix well with the cleaning product that had recently been used on the floors. Jeremiah pinched his nostrils and closed his eyes in disgust, but opened them again when an early student walked in, forcing him to squeeze under the partition to a new cubicle. By the time the bell rang, he was dying for a breath of fresh air.

On Tuesday he had been fearless, even in a crowded room. Today his blood ran cold when someone walked within six feet of him. It did no good to remind himself that no one could see him. He felt as if a neon sign flashed over his head saying THIEF!

Whatever had possessed him to boast about public education to his mother? His boasting had ended in this: thievery.

Jeremiah slunk along the corridors, sticking close to the walls. He ducked his head as he passed each doorway. He spied around corners before each turn. There was no sign of a supply room. There were pencils and textbooks in the teachers' lounge, but there were also teachers. The principal had a new box of typewriter paper on her desk, but Jeremiah didn't dare creep up and snatch it.

At last he went to Ruby's classroom and peered through the square of window in the door. If he told Ruby his problem and asked for help, would she be scandalized?

Ruby sat alone at her table. There were only five children in the room. Ms. McAllister was correcting papers, but from time to time she glanced up to see what Ruby and the other children were doing. The other children were whispering about Ruby, and Ruby was reading a book.

No one noticed when Jeremiah tiptoed into the room. No one noticed when his foot slipped and knocked against a bookshelf. But Jeremiah noticed what was on the shelf: dictionaries, reference books, and copies of the texts that Ruby used.

Jeremiah slipped a dictionary and three copies of each text into his paper bag. Also a heavy volume called a thesaurus that he hoped his mother might find useful. More than that he couldn't manage because his bag was getting heavy.

There was another paper bag standing open on Ruby's table. It was too small to carry books, or even a sandwich and an apple. On it was written EAT THIS, JAY!

Jeremiah lowered his own heavy bag to the floor and reached into Ruby's bag. It contained a musty mixture of ground-up leaves or herbs. He put a little on his tongue, then carefully wiped his tongue off with a pocket handkerchief. It tasted disgusting.

"Ruby Kourides!" Ms. McAllister called from her desk by the blackboard. "What is in that bag?"

Ruby looked at the table. Then she looked at the floor and noticed Jeremiah's bag. Jeremiah realized too late that since he no longer held it, it was visible. He considered picking it up again, but if it vanished while Ms. McAllister was watching, Ruby would be in more trouble than ever. He waited.

"What is in that bag?" Ms. McAllister repeated.

Ruby shrugged. "That big one? I don't know."

"You don't know? Then what is it doing there at your feet?"

Ms. McAllister pushed back her chair and walked across the room. After one glance into Jeremiah's bag her eyes widened with concern. "Ruby, dear—why?"

"Why what?" Ruby brushed a stray wisp of hair out of her eyes and squinted through her pale-rimmed glasses.

"Why did you take these books? You have text-books of your own. Why three more of each? And these reference books?"

Ruby shook her head, but Jeremiah could tell by the gleam in her eye that she had guessed how they got there.

"You know something about it, don't you?" Ms. McAllister persisted. "Has it something to do with your uncle? Did he tell you to bring books home from school?"

Jeremiah grew tense with indignation. Ms. McAllister, for all her friendly concern, seemed determined to get Ruby in trouble and show her uncle for a thief or a lunatic. But he would sooner get in trouble himself than let her get away with it. The moment she looked away, he snatched up the bag of books and quietly put each book where it belonged.

Meanwhile, Ms. McAllister picked up the small bag on the table, wrinkled her nose, and sniffed. "Ruby Kourides, what on earth is this?"

Ruby hesitated before answering: "Purslane, pokeweed, and rosemary."

"What for, dear? Is this your uncle's notion of a snack?"

Ruby's eyes flashed. "Ms. McAllister, what are you getting at? If you think my uncle is a thief or just plain crazy, why don't you say so?"

Ms. McAllister sighed, and again, for an instant, Jeremiah saw that she was just a nice woman who wanted the best for Ruby. If only she wasn't such a stupid woman, he thought. If only she would leave Ruby alone.

"I'm sorry," Ms. McAllister said. "I'm not accusing your uncle of anything, truly I'm not. But I can't understand why he would send you to school with a bag full of nasty-smelling herbs."

Ruby giggled. "When Uncle Homer and I are gone from this town, you know what's going to happen?"

Ms. McAllister smiled expectantly.

"You'll all be bored, that's what," said Ruby, and she went back to her book.

16

Once again, Ruby shared Jeremiah's lunch. She unpacked it on a bench in the playground: carrot sticks, a plum, a sandwich spread with blackberry preserves, and cookies.

"Aren't you hungry?" she asked.

Jeremiah took a carrot stick. "For this kind of thing I am. Why did you want me to eat those herbs?"

Ruby looked embarrassed. "Never mind. They probably wouldn't have worked."

"How were they supposed to work?"

"You heard what Uncle Homer said about things that made people reflect. I know he didn't mean that kind of reflection, but it was worth a try. Why don't you chew a little, just to see?"

Jeremiah's stomach flipped at the idea. "I don't want to see, and I don't want to be seen today," he said. "I'm the one who took those books and nearly got you into trouble."

Ruby ate slowly and methodically while Jeremiah repeated his conversation with his mother. Frowning in concentration, she nibbled the carrot sticks one by one. She unwrapped the sandwich and offered Jeremiah a bite. When he refused, she nibbled the crust around the edges before biting symmetrical scallops in what was left.

Jeremiah stopped talking to wipe the blackberry preserves off the part of his face where Ruby had guessed his mouth was. He looked doubtfully at his mother's homemade oatmeal cookies. He wasn't hungry, but if Ruby ate them, it would take her all day to finish at the rate she was going.

"Have some," Ruby said, thrusting out the bag. It hit him in the stomach, and most of the cookies were crushed. "What I don't understand is, why didn't you just say no?"

Jeremiah started to explain the difficulty of saying no to his mother, but Ruby interrupted him. "We need those books. I mean, the other students will, even after I leave. You can't just walk in and take them. It's not like the Friendly Neighbors bin, where people give things away."

Eating the plum took Ruby longer than all the rest combined. First she nibbled off small bits of skin and spat them into the lunch bag. Once the skin was removed, she ate the plum from the center out, a process that left most of the fruit around her nose and mouth.

After dropping the pit carefully into the bag and wiping first her face and then her glasses with a paper napkin, she finally stopped.

"Why so quiet?"

"I was watching you," Jeremiah said. "Why do you eat plums that peculiar way?"

"Do you like plum skins?" Ruby asked.

"I don't know. I guess I take bigger bites than you do, so I don't notice the skin part."

"Then you eat too fast, and that's bad for the digestion," Ruby informed him. "Plum skins are sour. Listen, I have an idea for your mother."

She led Jeremiah back inside the school, but instead of going toward the classrooms she went down some steps into a dimly lit area that smelled unused.

"Mr. James has a room down here," she explained. "Remember the first day you came? He's the janitor. Now, let me do the talking. He's nice enough, but you never know with grown-ups."

Jeremiah couldn't help admiring Ruby. She asked Mr. James all the right questions about his wife and kids, plus a few more that made him laugh. She said she didn't mind the smoke from his cigarettes, and almost looked as if she meant it. Slowly, she brought the conversation around to her departure for California.

"I'm going to hate it," she confided, and Jeremiah knew the tears in her eyes were genuine.

Mr. James ground his stub into an empty coffee mug, lit a second cigarette, and puffed thoughtfully. "None of my business, but I never did see the point of all this," he said. "Your uncle seems a decent guy. Not that I know him well, but he's always civil to me when I'm in his shop. Besides, plenty of kids are raised by a single parent these days. Nothing unusual about that."

"What's unusual is he's my uncle, not my father, and he's kind of old to be parenting, and the people in this town think he acts weird. You know that, so don't act stupid."

Jeremiah was shocked, but Mr. James chuckled. "I hope this new family of yours is used to kids who speak their mind. Anything I can do before you go, Ruby?"

"Funny you mentioned it," Ruby said. "There is."

A minute later, Jeremiah was following Ruby and Mr. James into a windowless room whose walls were lined with metal shelving. Stacked carelessly on the shelves were math books, science books, social studies books, even texts for beginning Spanish. The one thing all the books had in common was their battered state. Some had lost their bindings and some were trailing pages. All had been signed or drawn on countless times by countless students with leaky ballpoint pens.

"Pack them into one of those cardboard boxes in the corner there," said Mr. James. "Take as many as you like—they won't be missed. Only reason I haven't thrown them out is you need a letter of permission to throw out anything in this school. I'm afraid they're not in tip-top condition."

"They'll do," said Ruby. "I'll come back for them when school lets out."

Her face was triumphant as she led Jeremiah back to the playground. He was glad for once that she couldn't see his own face. He knew it couldn't look enthusiastic. What would his mother say when he brought home a box full of textbooks that were more worn out than the books she had already? And he still hadn't found any paper or pencils.

"Thanks, Ruby," he said all the same. "I bet you miss Mr. James when you're gone, even if you don't miss the other kids in the school."

Ruby shrugged. "It's not so much that I won't miss them. It's knowing they won't miss *me*. I'm nothing to them—an absolute zero. I wish for once I could do something to impress them, like in sports, for instance. Do you think you could teach me to shoot baskets?"

"Shoot?" Jeremiah repeated. He felt confused.

Ruby grinned shyly. "You heard me. Why do you think there was hardly anyone left in the classroom? It was sports period and they were playing basketball, that's why. The other kids you saw had colds. I pretended I had one, too, because I miss so often that it's getting to be a joke. Could you teach me how?"

"I'm not very good at sports," said Jeremiah. "It's all I can do to climb the cedar tree outside Mr. Sweeny's house, and that's with fifty years of practice."

They watched as some children lined up to shoot baskets. A girl younger than Jeremiah shot four in a row. An older boy got up to eight.

"I wish I could do that," Ruby said. "I wish I could shoot a dozen. Maybe two dozen. Maybe even ninety-nine."

Suddenly Jeremiah had an idea. He couldn't help Ruby, but he knew who could. Mike O'Malley was good at sports and so were the twins. Even April and Jessie weren't too bad. If they all got together, they could make sure Ruby's ball got into the net, and the children from Athens Elementary would never know how she did it.

"Listen, Ruby," he said excitedly, "I think I can help you after all. Not right now, but tomorrow. Tell those kids you'll shoot as many baskets as they like, and you won't miss a single one."

Ruby's face lit up. "Really? You're wonderful! Now they'll remember me as something else besides the girl with the crazy uncle."

17

"Here he is now!"

One look at his mother's face was enough to make Jeremiah want to drop the box of books and run. It was pink with pride. Sitting across from her at the kitchen table were Mr. and Mrs. O'Malley, whose faces were supposed to be green with envy. Jeremiah had to admit that at least they looked impressed.

"Show us, darling."

Jeremiah moved into the room. What were the O'Malleys doing there? The two families had never been close friends. If Dr. and Mrs. Anderson came to call, for instance, his mother would serve coffee in her china cups, in the parlor. She would bring out her blackberry preserves. When the O'Malleys came, they got their coffee in mugs at the kitchen table, and the preserves remained in the cupboard.

"Don't be bashful, Jeremiah." Mrs. Jenkins turned to her neighbors and smiled. "You won't believe this, but he didn't want me to spread the good news. He hates to boast, unlike the other children. But I think a child should get the praise he deserves, don't you?"

Jeremiah set the box on the kitchen table. To his surprise, he saw there was something to eat after all, but not the sort of thing his mother would serve. She believed in homemade desserts, with as little refined sugar as possible. The plate of Hostess Twinkies must have been brought by the O'Malleys.

Mrs. Jenkins leaned over the box. The change in her expression was so abrupt that Jeremiah couldn't hold back a little gasp that was close to laughter. "Sorry," he said. "It was all there was."

"All there was! Do you mean to say the children of Athens, Connecticut—which has one of the finest school systems in the country, mind you—study from books like these? Why, they're unsanitary!"

With a ladylike shudder she lifted a textbook by the spine, dropped it on the table, and wiped her fingers on a napkin. "This one isn't even in English."

"It's Spanish," Jeremiah informed her. "Beginning Spanish."

"So I see. Well, dear, no one can blame you. After all, you're doing this with no help whatsoever from the other children, but I'm afraid you let your attention stray. These are obviously discarded texts. If you keep on looking, you'll find new ones."

"I did," said Jeremiah. "I couldn't take them. Ruby said the students needed them."

"You're a student, aren't you?" Mrs. Jenkins pursed her lips before letting her breath out in a long, slow sigh. "Have you said hello to Mr. and Mrs. O'Malley? They've been kind enough to bring you a treat. No, don't take one now, dear. It would spoil your appetite for supper."

Supper was hours away, and Jeremiah knew that even after eating the nutritious meal his mother had prepared that day, he still would not be allowed a Hostess Twinkie.

"What else did you bring? Paper? Notebooks? Pencils?"

Jeremiah fumbled in his shirt pocket and drew out something made of wire and pink plastic. "Only this."

Again his mother leaned forward, and again her expression turned to disgust. "What is it?"

"I don't know." Jeremiah examined it, shook his head, and slipped it back into his pocket. "I thought it might come in useful. It was in the trash can, in the lunchroom."

"Trash can! What were you doing in the trash can?"

Jeremiah stared at her in disbelief. For fifty years, he and the other children in Pineapple Place had gone through trash cans every chance they got. So had their parents, for that matter. Rag-bagging was necessary to their existence, and his mother knew it perfectly well.

"I was looking for pencils," he said. "All I found

was stubs, though. Every single eraser was bitten off, and they all had tooth marks. The only place we're going to find new pencils is a store."

His mother looked annoyed. Not just annoyed—embarrassed. She obviously thought she had lost face with the O'Malleys, and Jeremiah felt sorry for her. "I can go back tomorrow," he said reluctantly.

"You can go back today."

"I can't," said Jeremiah. "School got out at three."

"Then hurry. It's only twenty past, and they won't be locking up for a while yet. Get clean books this time. And if there are no pencils, take some chalk."

Jeremiah took a deep breath before saying shakily, "I think we were wrong about the school supplies. I mean, not just you—me, too. I don't think they count as free education. They're not free at all for us, and if I take them I'll just get Ruby into trouble."

He noticed a glint of tears in his mother's eyes and shifted his weight awkwardly from one leg to the other. "I guess I could go back and see, though," he said at last. "It's just I'm not sure—"

Mrs. O'Malley stood up quickly, jarring the kitchen table so that coffee sloshed out of the mugs. "Of course you're sure, sweetheart. Your mother knows best, doesn't she? Why, just before you came in she showed us in a book where it says public education isn't just a right, it's been the law in parts of New England as far back as 1642. Or was it 1462?"

"It was both," her husband said decisively. "So

it's not just your right to get us supplies, it's your duty. And while you're at it, we have a small favor to ask. It concerns our Meggie.''

"Meggie?" Jeremiah looked at him doubtfully.

"Her birthday is coming up next week," Mrs. O'Malley reminded him. "She'll be five."

Jeremiah giggled. "She's already five. She's been five for fifty years."

"That's just it," Mr. O'Malley said, smiling sadly. "Fifty years, and since we left Baltimore she's never had a doll that didn't come from the trash."

"We've heard there's a kind called Cabbage Patch," Mrs. O'Malley continued. "I think I spotted one when I was out walking the other day. Adorable! Just right for Meggie."

Jeremiah's heart sank. He knew what was coming next.

"Isn't there a baby class in your school?" Mr. O'Malley asked. "A what-do-you-call-it—winter-garden?"

"There might be," said Jeremiah. "I didn't notice."

"If you could just slip in and take a quick look."

Jeremiah glanced regretfully at the forbidden Twinkies. They were poor payment for what the O'Malleys asked. "You mean take one of those cabbage dolls? I don't even know what they look like. Besides, I couldn't steal one from a little kid."

Mr. O'Malley laughed heartily. "Steal one? No,

no, no! That's the whole point. Wintergardens have toys that children share. Meggie went to a baby class in Baltimore, fifty years back. The kiddies played with dolls in school, but they weren't allowed to bring them home.''

"Then I'm not either," said Jeremiah.

"You are if it's for special education," Mr. O'Malley assured him. "Your mother just explained it to us. We can't send the kiddies to school, so the school sends supplies to us."

"It's stealing, not sending," Jeremiah said. "If you want that doll, get one of your own kids to take it. They're invisible, too, aren't they?"

Both O'Malleys shook their heads. "Not always. Our clan holds the record for being seen."

Jeremiah smiled at the pride in their faces. So much for being green with envy!

"We think this should be your job," Mrs. O'Malley explained. "If one of our clan is caught, it might make trouble. We don't want word of this getting to Mr. Sweeny, do we?"

There was a hint of a threat in her voice, and Jeremiah realized he was being blackmailed. "I'll see what I can do," he said.

Before he had time to shut the front door behind him, Jeremiah caught sight of Mr. Todd across the street. He could hardly help noticing him: the mysterious beckonings and anxious glances to the left and right as Mr. Todd leaned out his window were enough to attract anyone's attention.

"Come over here, boy!" he whispered hoarsely. "Tell me, how was school?"

"Okay, I guess. I've only been there twice."

"So I heard." Mr. Todd nodded meaningfully at Mrs. Pettylittle's house. "A little bird told me. In the strictest secrecy, of course."

Jeremiah wondered if there were anybody Mrs. Pettylittle had not told. "I went to sixth grade," he said. "They're doing the Middle Ages. It was fun."

"Splendid! Bells or buzzers?"

"Neither," Jeremiah said. "It was thanes and churls, and the bubonic plague."

Mr. Todd shook with the same suspiciously hearty laugh that Mr. O'Malley had produced a few minutes earlier. It sounded just as fake. "No, no, no!" he gasped. "I'm speaking of the clocks. Every classroom has a clock, right?"

Jeremiah nodded. "I think so."

"Well, when the hour is over, when it's time for lunch, or sports, or the end of school, do they ring or do they buzz?"

"They ring."

"Splendid!" Mr. Todd repeated. "Get me one."

Jeremiah smiled politely. "I don't understand."

"A clock with a bell contraption in it," Mr. Todd explained, his voice sharp with impatience. "You may have to disconnect a few wires, but you've watched me do that often enough. Disconnect them at the far end if you can—I'm running low on wires."

Jeremiah took a deep breath. Was the man serious? "I don't think I could do that. I have a feeling it isn't legal."

"Legal? It's allocation of public funds for the handicapped. What's more legal than that?"

"Bells and wires aren't exactly public funds," Jeremiah objected. "Besides, it means climbing up high. What am I supposed to do, borrow a stepladder from the janitor?"

Mr. Todd chuckled. "Climbing is old hat for you, isn't it, boy? I've seen you in that cedar tree, listening at Sweeny's window. You wouldn't want word to get out about that now, would you?" Mr. Todd winked before turning away.

Jeremiah groaned when he saw Mrs. Anderson waiting for him on her front steps as he went by. Mrs. Anderson was his favorite grown-up in Pineapple Place. She treated him as if he were April's younger brother, and sometimes even took his side in an argument. He hoped she wasn't going to ask him for something from Athens Elementary.

"Could you come in a minute, dear? Someone wants to talk to you."

"April?" Jeremiah asked hopefully.

"April is out rag-bagging with the other children. Not that she expects to find much—this town is so clean it's enough to try the patience of a saint. No, it's the doctor who wants a word with you."

Dr. Anderson was in the room he called his laboratory, a room that served as a pantry in the other houses on the street. He was dressed in the same white tunic and pants he had worn for fifty years in his relentless search for a cure for the common cold.

"Hello there!" he said, looking up from a row of test tubes. "I hear you've been to school."

"Did a little bird tell you?"

Dr. Anderson's hazel eyes twinkled with the same twinkle April's eyes had when she was in a good mood. "Mrs. Pettylittle told me. How was it? Bring back anything useful?"

"I didn't go to rag-bag," Jeremiah said. "I went to learn. I learned some cures for the bubonic plague, in case you're interested. And I found this. Do you know what it is?"

Dr. Anderson studied the wire-and-plastic object that Jeremiah pulled from his pocket. "Fascinating, the progress we make over the years," he said at last. "Lightweight, and easily cleaned. Removable as well."

"What is it?" Jeremiah asked.

"An orthodontic device for straightening teeth. Where did you find it?"

"In the lunchroom trash can, wrapped in a napkin."

Dr. Anderson handed it back. "On second thought, maybe removable isn't progress. Better return it to the child who threw it out. Now, I'll get straight to the point. Does this school have an infirmary?"

"Infirmary?" The sinking feeling returned to Jeremiah's chest.

"You know, a nurse's office. A sickroom. Whatever. Could you find out?"

"Why?" asked Jeremiah.

"Don't panic—this is a good cause. It's been years since I had a supply of sterile bandages. That's one thing you rag-baggers will never find in the trash."

Jeremiah's hands flew to his ears as the doctor produced the same hearty laugh he had just heard twice before. He refused even to smile in return. "What's happened to all you guys? Why don't you just ask me to hold up the school? Then I could get the kids' lunch money and the principal's purse. And you haven't mentioned Mr. Sweeny yet."

Dr. Anderson looked dazed. "Mr. Sweeny? What about him?"

"You're supposed to remind me how I wouldn't like him to know I've been to school," said Jeremiah. "You know, just to make sure I get you what you want."

As Mrs. Anderson hustled him out of the laboratory, Jeremiah thought he could hear the doctor murmuring, "No, no, no!"

These were the words he used himself when he stepped into the street and was confronted by April and all five O'Malley children.

"There he is!" said Mike. "Jeremiah, we need lunch boxes."

"One apiece," Jessie specified, "and no cute pictures on mine, please. I want mine plain."

Jeremiah stared at her. "Where am I supposed to get six lunch boxes?"

142

"School, of course. Don't play dumb."

"Get them yourself," said Jeremiah. "What's wrong with you? Growing lazy after all these years?"

"We're just being discreet," April explained. Her voice was firm, but there was a twinkle in her eye. "You wanted to keep Athens Elementary to yourself. Well, that's okay with us, but we need lunch boxes. With thermos bottles inside, to keep our cocoa hot in the North Pole."

Jeremiah let out a sigh of relief. "Is that why? Then you can forget it. I'm solving the trash-flow problem, so we won't have to go."

"That's what you think," April said. "We're moving first thing in the morning. Mrs. Sweeny brought a notice around to all our parents. So how about getting us those lunch boxes?"

"No!" Jeremiah shouted. "No, no, no!"

He ran back to his house and spent the rest of the afternoon sitting at the back of his closet.

18

Night turned the streets into new patterns of light and shadow. Each street lamp was a separate sun, and the distances from lamp to lamp were starless stretches of space.

Jeremiah stayed in the shadows. Not that he feared being seen, but he wasn't in the mood for light and the cheer it offered. He had gone all the way into town at ten o'clock, but Ruby wasn't home. A dim light shone behind the counter at the back of the pharmacy, but the door was locked. Everything was dark upstairs, and no one came when he knocked.

The night air was warm for mid-October. A soft wind flipped the leaves pale-side up, as though it were about to rain. Some of the leaves dropped from their branches and swirled away like giant moths, or bats. A single black Labrador slunk along behind him, approaching to nudge him from time to time, but Jeremiah kept his hands in his pockets. He wasn't in the mood to pat a dog; Ruby had not been home.

Ahead half a block or so, close to the entrance to Pineapple Place, a dark shape appeared. It moved slowly toward him, hesitated for a moment, then moved again more quickly. It was Mrs. Pettylittle.

"Jeremiah, can that be you?"

He didn't answer, but the dog growled and trotted away.

"Odd, isn't it?" said Mrs. Pettylittle. "I'm fond of dogs, but dogs aren't fond of me—whereas they follow the rest of you around. Do you suppose they're attracted to invisibility?"

"I don't know and I don't care," said Jeremiah. "I'm not afraid of them anymore. It's just I was thinking about something else."

Mrs. Pettylittle came closer and peered into his face. "Have you been crying?"

One minute he hated her, and the next he threw his arms around her waist.

"What's wrong?"

"Everything!" he gasped. "Just everything!"

Mrs. Pettylittle held him for a moment before pulling away. "Let's walk around the block and you can tell me what happened."

"We're moving, that's what happened. I'm solving the trash-flow problem, so why is Mr. Sweeny moving us away?"

"Who says he is?" Mrs. Pettylittle asked.

"April. She says first thing in the morning. But I

wanted to go back to school and find out more about the Middle Ages. And I promised Ruby I'd help her shoot baskets during recess. Now I can't even find her to explain.''

"They went to Flo's for supper," Mrs. Pettylittle said. "I was with them, and we stayed a little late. I'm surprised you didn't pass them on your way home.''

"I didn't pass anyone," Jeremiah said, wiping his eyes and nose on his knit sleeve. "Only dogs.''

"Then they're still there. They were chatting with Flo when I started back.''

"So you got a chance to say good-bye," Jeremiah said gloomily.

"Actually, it didn't occur to me. I don't think Mr. Sweeny really means to move us. If you want my opinion, it was just an idle threat.''

"I'm tired of threats," said Jeremiah. "He's not the only one to threaten, either. There's hardly anyone in the whole of Pineapple Place who doesn't want something from me.''

Mrs. Pettylittle walked slowly, bending toward Jeremiah as he described the O'Malleys' visit to his mother's kitchen. When he mentioned the Cabbage Patch doll she smiled, but when he told her about Mr. Todd and his request for a clock with a bell that rang, complete with wires, she shook her head and made a clucking sound.

"If sterile bandages were needed, *I* should have been asked," she said when his story was finished. "Homer will give me some if I ask. But the O'Malleys are just plain silly, and as for Theophilus Todd—why, I'm surprised at him!''

She sounded calm and confident, but what if she never got a chance to ask Ruby's uncle for bandages? What if Jeremiah climbed the cedar tree the next morning and, rather than Long Island Sound, saw a sea of ice? What if he never met Ruby again? Not just never in the eighty years or so a normal man would live. Never forever.

"Could we go back to Flo's, please?" he asked. "I don't care what you think, I'd feel better if I said good-bye."

They had walked all the way around the block and were approaching Pineapple Place once more from the other side. The wind had died down, and the night air had shriveled into a silent chill. Stars that had not been visible earlier glinted overhead. Far away a dog howled, and even farther, another dog answered him.

Mrs. Pettylittle stopped and gazed at the sidewalk for a while. Then she squeezed Jeremiah's hand. "It's not fair for me to tell you why until I'm really sure, but I want you to stop worrying about the North Pole. We probably won't go at all, and we definitely won't go tomorrow morning because Mr. Sweeny needs supplies before he moves us anywhere, and that means another trip to the dump. So you can slip out early and help Ruby shoot those baskets. All right?"

"No," said Jeremiah. "As long as I'm a prisoner in this place, nothing will ever be all right again."

The Fifth Day

19

They drew straws, and Bessie was the one to climb the pole. Mike gave her a leg up, holding her steady as she stopped to giggle, hitch up her multicolored knit skirt, and wave at her twin sister.

"Kick off your shoes," he advised. "No one can shinny in shoes."

"Someone has to catch them then," said Bessie. "If I'm not wearing them, they'll be visible."

The shoes became visible for a split second between the time Bessie kicked them off and Mike caught them.

"Here goes!" Bessie cried.

But her feet in their rainbow socks could no longer grip at all. She slid down, put the socks in her pocket, and began again barefoot.

"Hurry!" Jeremiah hissed at her, with an anxious glance toward the school.

"Hold your horses!" Mike grumbled. "You're lucky we're doing this at all."

"Yes, considering how sneaky you were," Tessie agreed. "If you find a friend, you're not supposed to keep her to yourself. You're supposed to share."

"Only if we like her, of course," Bessie gasped from halfway up the pole.

But April looked curiously at Jeremiah and asked, "Will we like her? Do you think she'll like me?"

Suddenly Jeremiah clenched his teeth so tight that it hurt every muscle in his jaw and neck. He knew they would all like Ruby. The problem was, he suspected Ruby would like April and the other children from Pineapple Place more than she liked Jeremiah himself. Who, in the past fifty years, had not liked the others better? Only his own mother, and she didn't count.

He looked at the other children from Pineapple Place and, in spite of himself, was proud to know Ruby would like them. They teased him, but they were a loyal bunch. It was too bad Ruby couldn't get to know them better. But soon he would be in the North Pole and Ruby would be in California, and no one would care how many baskets had been shot at Athens Elementary on a Friday morning in October, or whether the players had made friends after the game. Then he remembered that although the other children from Pineapple Place might see and like Ruby, she couldn't see or like them back.

Even if he had wanted to, he wouldn't have been able to share.

A bell rang inside the school and children filed out for recess.

"Ruby is the one with the braids and glasses," he said. "She isn't any good at sports. Do you think we can pull this off?"

"Piece of cake," Mike boasted. "The only hard part is making it look as if she threw the ball."

Ruby moved toward the basketball court, followed by a group of classmates. There was a worried look on her face. She kept taking her glasses off to wipe them on her skirt, then putting them back on to blink anxiously at the net. She looked around her, as if searching for Jeremiah. She slipped the mirror from her pocket, but immediately slipped it in again. Jeremiah waved at her from his position under the net. She stared right through him.

"I'm over here!" he called.

She turned in his direction, smiled, and seemed to relax. "I was afraid you'd forgotten. Quick, tell me what to do!"

A girl he recognized from Ms. McAllister's class thought Ruby had been talking to her. "What do you mean, tell you what to do? You told us you'd shoot ninety-nine baskets, Ruby Kourides. In a row! I've never even seen you shoot two in a row. Are you crazy or something?"

"Wait and see," said Ruby.

Mike O'Malley stood six feet away from Jeremiah, to the left of the net. He showed April where to stand opposite him, on the right. Tessie was stationed farther back, where she could catch the ball if the others missed.

"Let's get this straight," Mike said. "This Ruby friend of yours can't see you but she can hear you, right?"

"Not exactly," said Jeremiah. "She can see me in mirrors."

"That's not the point. Can the others hear you, too?"

"Of course not."

"Then I'll tell you what to do, and you can tell her. Tell her not to hurry, whatever she does. As long as she takes her time and doesn't panic, we can get the ball into the net. But tell her she was a fool to say she'd do it."

"Ruby's no fool," said Jeremiah.

Mike flashed him a grin. "Ready?"

"Ready?" Jeremiah relayed to Ruby.

"Ready," Ruby said.

"Okay," said Jeremiah. "Now, the trick is not to hurry, whatever you do. Take your time and don't panic. You were in a panic when you tried before, weren't you?"

Ruby nodded.

"Well, don't. Stay calm and I promise you won't miss."

Ruby put the basketball on the ground and held it between her ankles while she fastened her braids together behind her head by putting one braid inside the rubber band that held the other. She polished her glasses one last time. She spat on her hands, rubbed them together, then wiped them on her skirt.

"Quit stalling, Ruby," said the girl from Ms. McAllister's classroom.

Ruby picked up the ball, squinted, aimed, shot, and almost made the basket. All Bessie had to do was gently nudge it over the rim.

"One," said Ruby. She sounded surprised.

After taking a deep breath, she hopped from one foot to the other and aimed again. This time the ball went in. Ruby looked astonished. "Two!" she said.

The third time the ball went to the side. Bessie barely caught it and, once she did, nearly lost her grip on the pole.

"That's funny," said one of the boys who was watching. "I thought for sure she was going to miss."

"Three," said Ruby with a growing tone of confidence.

Up went the ball a fourth time. It came down short of the net but Mike reached out and gave it a tap toward April, who sent it on its way to Bessie.

"Four!"

The crowd was impressed. Not because it was unusual to shoot four baskets in a row, but because they had been shot by Ruby Kourides.

"There's something weird about that ball," said the boy who had thought it would miss on the third time around.

"It went in, didn't it?" Ruby challenged him.

He nodded doubtfully.

"Here goes five," said Ruby.

She threw the ball without so much as a glance at the net since she was still glaring at the boy. The ball went astray, but Mike leapt out and caught it just before it hit the ground. Jumping high, he tried to shoot the basket himself, but missed. Bessie missed, too, and the ball fell down again to be caught by Jeremiah, who panicked in spite of his advice to Ruby and threw it at Tessie. Tessie sent it back up to her twin, who calmly shoved it through the net.

"Five," said Ruby.

Mike pulled a fat gold watch—one of Mr. Todd's creations—from his knit pocket. "How many more minutes does recess last?"

"Fifteen," said Jeremiah.

"No, just five," said Ruby. "Ninety-four left to go."

"Wait a minute!" Mike put his hands on his hips and scowled at Jeremiah. "What does she mean by 'ninety-four'?"

Jeremiah remembered how he had told Ruby she could shoot as many baskets as she liked. Inwardly, he groaned. "I guess she boasted that she could shoot ninety-nine in a row," he whispered. "I'm afraid it's my fault."

"She'll never make it," Mike announced. "Better give up."

"You'll never make it," Jeremiah relayed to Ruby. "Better give up."

"Give up?" Ruby fixed him with a stormy glare. "Just when I got the hang of it? You can't!"

"Who are you talking to?" asked the girl from Ms. McAllister's class. "I don't know what's going on, but it looks like cheating. The ball is supposed to go straight into the net. That last time it bounced."

"It did not," said Ruby.

"It did."

"Ruby's right," said someone else. "It almost hit the ground, but it went back up again."

"So it doesn't count."

"Yes, it does. It's weird, but it counts."

While they argued, Ruby aimed again.

"Hold it!" Mike shouted.

It was too late. Ruby had already thrown the ball, which would have gone straight into the net if Bessie hadn't caught it.

"What's the matter?" Bessie asked.

"I don't know if we should go on with this or not," said Mike. "It's a waste of time. What does it prove?"

"I don't know," said Bessie. "Hurry up and decide. My legs are beginning to ache."

"Of course we should go on," said April. "Jeremiah promised, didn't he?"

"Yes, but he didn't ask us first."

"Please go on!" Jeremiah begged them.

"I can't," said Ruby. "I can't see the ball."

"She can't see the ball," Jeremiah told Mike.

"Bessie, let go!" Mike hollered. "When you're holding it like that it disappears, remember?"

Bessie let the ball drop but caught it again before it hit the net. "I'm sick of this!" she cried. "It's going to take forever to get up to ninety-nine."

While she argued with Mike, she let the ball drop and caught it again repeatedly, so that for Ruby and her classmates it flashed on and off like a blinking traffic light.

The playground was silent for a few seconds before the children began to murmur and then shout. One child accused Ruby of filling the ball with helium. Another blamed it on the weather. A rumor went around that the ball was suspended from a string tied to the flagpole, but the theory was vetoed since the flagpole was at least a hundred yards away.

"Let go," Jeremiah told Bessie.

"I did," said Ruby. "It's up there over the net, but it's kind of stuck."

"Throw a stone at it!" said the girl from Ms. McAllister's class.

When Jeremiah saw several students lean down to pick up stones, he went cold with fear. "Get down, Bessie!" he shouted. "Drop that ball and get away from there or you'll be hurt. And that goes for the rest of you, too!"

A look of sudden understanding spread over Ruby's face. Her arms dropped limply to her sides, as if they had come loose from their sockets. "It wasn't me who shot those baskets after all," she whispered. "You cheated, and you made me cheat. I hate you, Jay Jenkins!"

Jeremiah was stunned. Shame and confusion flooded up inside him until he felt hot all over. "Then you won't miss me, will you?" he said stiffly. "That's good, because we're leaving after all. Mr. Sweeny is taking us to the North Pole, and I'll never see you again."

20

Jeremiah followed the street the school was on all the way to the end. As Ruby had told him two days earlier, there was a swampy stretch of shore where, if he pushed through the rushes, he could sit in a quiet place near the water. He felt terrible, and he missed Ruby.

Why hadn't she appreciated the joke he and the other children from Pineapple Place had played to fool her classmates? It was just like the time he had tried to help her with her math problem. Instead of being grateful, she was angry.

Jeremiah settled with his back against a rock. The rock felt warm, even through his knit shirt. A few feet away the marsh grass stopped, giving way to a stretch of mud. Beyond the mud, water lay in a silver sheet that moved in little shivers as the tide came in. A heron stood motionless on one leg in the shallow water. The leg continued in its own reflection, ending in a second heron that was upside down and also motionless. Jeremiah watched until it stabbed at a minnow and flew off with awkward flaps of its wide wings, croaking in a voice too ugly for its body.

Ruby liked this place. "I'll take you there one day," she had said. But now they weren't friends anymore. What if he went back and apologized? What if he said, "Ruby, for us it's fun. It's the only kind of fun we can have, most of the time." Would she understand? Or was her outside world hopelessly different from the inside world of Pineapple Place?

Before he could imagine her answer, a shadow fell across him. "What are you doing here?" asked Mrs. Jenkins.

Jeremiah was astonished. His mother rarely left Pineapple Place to venture into the outside world. When she did, she stuck to the commercial parts of town where she could window-shop.

"I went out looking for you," she explained. "I went to find that school, and you were just walking away from it."

Come to think of it, she didn't look as out of place at the waterfront as he would have expected. Wisps of dark hair had escaped from her bun, and she kept brushing them back when the breeze blew them across her eyes. She had knotted the sleeves of one of Mrs. Anderson's multicolored sweaters around her shoulders. For a moment Jeremiah imagined her as a big sister rather than a mother.

"I passed the other children on my way," she told

him. "Those O'Malleys were laughing like hyenas. What's wrong? Did they play some kind of prank on you?"

"We played it together," Jeremiah said. "We thought we were helping Ruby shoot baskets, but she said it was cheating so she got mad instead."

"Ruby!" Mrs. Jenkins reached down and pulled him to his feet. With a gentle but firm grip on his elbow, she propelled him over the marsh grass, carefully picking her way between the rocks. "For fifty years you stay out of trouble, and now that you've been seen by that girl, everything goes topsy-turvy. You've not the same old Jeremiah anymore."

Jeremiah found the crossness in her face unconvincing. She still had an older sister look about her. He pulled away from her grasp. "I'm glad I'm not. I want to be just plain Jay."

"Jay?" His mother looked bewildered. Then she smiled. "So you want to be Jay, like your father. Well, why not? After all, you're the spitting image of him."

Jeremiah caught his breath. "My father? I thought his name was Jeremiah, like mine."

"So it was," Mrs. Jenkins said, "but he wanted a no-nonsense name, so he shortened it to Jay. He said that suited him better. Maybe it suits you better, too. As I said, you're the spitting image, except perhaps for your eyes. They're more like mine."

Jeremiah blinked his eyes. "Am I a no-nonsense person?"

"You're stubborn, and you seem to know what you want and how to get it." She frowned, and then chuckled.

Jeremiah stopped walking and waited until his mother stopped, too, and was forced to come back to stand beside him.

"Aren't you coming?" she asked.

"I'm coming," said Jeremiah. "Just tell me this, first. Weren't you ever seen?"

Mrs. Jenkins brushed the wisps of hair out of her eyes again. "Once. Only once."

"Tell me about it."

"Oh, there isn't much to tell," she said. "I was window-shopping in Kansas City, and another woman saw me in the reflection. She spoke to me, and I don't know what came over me, but I answered. She could hear me, too."

"But that's just like me and Ruby!" Jeremiah said excitedly.

His mother nodded. "It isn't at all the way the others have been seen. It must run in the family."

"Well, then what happened?"

"Nothing. We talked for a long time, that's all. She wasn't frightened, even when she bumped into me by accident. I told her about the way we live, and she told me things about herself."

"So you were friends."

Mrs. Jenkins shook her head. "I wanted to be. We planned to meet again, in front of the same store. But that night Mr. Sweeny moved us out of Kansas City."

"Then don't you understand about Ruby?" Jeremiah asked. "Don't you see why we mustn't move away?"

"I don't know what's going to happen to us, Jeremiah," his mother said. "I honestly don't. Mr. Sweeny is very upset. Mrs. Pettylittle happened to mention how that dreadful pharmacist gave you something to make you visible, and it put him in a state such as I've never seen before. That's why I came to find you. He has called a general meeting."

21

"I don't hold with introducing foreign substances into the body," Mr. Sweeny said. "I never did, and I never will. It's unnatural."

Dr. Anderson looked closely at Jeremiah. "It doesn't seem to have done him any harm," he remarked.

Mr. Sweeny made a noise halfway between spitting and choking. "No harm? Don't be stupid, Anderson. This man who calls himself a pharmacist has exposed the child to the crowds, the rabble, the hoi polloi, everybody and his uncle. He had to be fetched from a police station, of all things. Who knows what the future ill effects will be? Visibility potions—what next!"

"You should have come to us," Mrs. Jenkins told her son in a shaky voice. "We all understand that it wasn't your fault, but you should have come straight home."

"I did," said Jeremiah.

He looked around Mr. Sweeny's living room, letting his eyes rest briefly on the members of the older generation. His mother and Mrs. Sweeny stood side by side, their faces tense with worry. Mr. Todd sat in a corner, deathly still except for his eyes, which sparkled with malicious glee. His mother's eyes sparkled, too, but with tears. The O'Malley parents, generally lenient, were quivering with shocked delight that Jeremiah, rather than one of their own rowdy brood, was in deep trouble.

"I did come home," Jeremiah said. "Home wasn't here. I couldn't see any of you. I couldn't see Pineapple Place at all. I thought you had moved away."

"Which is precisely what we're going to do," Mr. Sweeny grunted as he shifted his weight in the armchair, where his wife had tucked him in with two wool blankets. "You'd better start thinking *cold!*"

A murmur rose from the open window, where April and the O'Malley children jostled one another as they tried to see into the room.

Jeremiah had never seen Mr. Sweeny in such a temper. He felt like running to his mother for protection, but he forced himself to walk up to the armchair. "That's not fair," he said. "You said to solve the trash-flow problem, and I did. I got you clothes, and books, and all sorts of household things, and I can get you sterile bandages, too. Ruby's uncle could give us all sorts of things for Dr. Anderson. Can't we wait a few more days?"

166

Mr. Sweeny's eyes flashed with anger. "Ruby's uncle! What business did you have with Ruby's uncle, if I may ask? I take it he's the so-called pharmacist."

"He's a real pharmacist," Jeremiah protested. "It's just he uses herbs, but you shouldn't mind that, because herbs aren't foreign substances. At least, not like drugs. He and Ruby are the nicest people I've met in fifty years. And that includes you!"

The murmur at the window ceased. Jeremiah turned to look at the awestruck faces of the other children from Pineapple Place. To his knowledge, not one of them had ever stood up to Mr. Sweeny. Suddenly he stopped feeling so afraid. In fact, he felt like laughing.

"I'm sorry, sir," he said in an effort to appease the old man. "But the others have all been seen before, so why not me?"

"The others were seen by pure chance," Mr. Sweeny snapped. "Never once has one of us been made visible because he was spoon-fed pepper and parsley by a meddlesome crank who sets himself up as a pharmacist."

"I tell you, he is a pharmacist," Jeremiah insisted. "He has diplomas on his wall. And it wasn't pepper and parsley. Besides, how could I have helped it?"

"You said herbs, didn't you? Kindly stop contradicting me." Mr. Sweeny pulled the wool blankets up to his chin and glared at his wife. "Close that window, woman. Did you think we were in Florida?"

Mrs. Sweeny hurried to the window and slammed

it down. On the other side, April and the O'Malley children made worried gestures. Jeremiah ignored them.

"You asked how you could have helped it," Mr. Sweeny continued. "Well, I'm telling you. You could have minded your own business, and that's what you'll do from now on or I'll ground you for the next hundred years. For a whole century you wouldn't set foot outside of Pineapple Place. How would you like that, eh?"

"It wouldn't make much difference," Jeremiah answered. "I'm already a prisoner here."

Again he looked around the living room. To his surprise, a new feeling surged up inside him: affection. He realized that he actually liked them all, every last one of them, including Mr. Sweeny. In fact, he loved them.

"I guess we're all prisoners," he said. "I just didn't notice before, because it used to be fun. Then it stopped being fun anymore, because everybody changed. My mother got fussier, and the other kids got teasier, and Mr. Sweeny got into a bad mood. Everybody wanted something from me. Why did you all change?"

Mr. Sweeny leaned forward in his chair and roared. "Look who's talking! I thought you were the one who wanted to change. I understand you've been to school, all on your own."

Jeremiah looked reproachfully at the other grown-ups in the room. Which one had told?

"No one tattled," Mr. Sweeny said, reading Jeremiah's mind. "I don't get my information from little birds, I get it from my own superior brainpower. Athens Elementary, indeed! You'd better put on an extra pair of socks, because we're leaving for the North Pole.''

A startled cry came from the children at the far side of the window, but it had nothing to do with Mr. Sweeny's last words. They were looking at something in the street. A moment later the door flew open and a stranger walked in.

''Sorry for the intrusion,'' Homer Kourides said quietly, ''but what's all this nonsense about the North Pole?''

22

Mr. Sweeny behaved the way Jeremiah imagined a volcano might behave during the last few seconds before an explosion. First he rumbled. Then he shook. His face grew darker as his eyes grew brighter. But just before the explosion, he simmered down.

"How did you get here?" he asked in a weary voice.

"Spurge, and celandine, and alder buckthorn, mainly," said Homer Kourides. "They work on warts, so it follows that in larger quantities they work on the whole body. A simple matter of making me and Ruby disappear for the rest of the world. I'd be interested in hearing how you did it yourself fifty years ago."

"None of your business," said Mr. Sweeny.

"Not true," Homer Kourides disagreed. "How did you make it last? Unless Ruby and I take regular doses, we'll start materializing fairly soon."

"The sooner the better," Mr. Sweeny said.

"Now, my visibility potion was a different matter. It was tricky, making someone materialize who wasn't there to start with," Homer Kourides continued. "I spilled most of the stuff before I found the young man's mouth."

"Nobody asked you to find his mouth," Mr. Sweeny grumbled. "Your own fault if it spilled."

"No harm done. I made another batch."

Homer Kourides smiled at the other grown-ups in the room. "Hello, Letty!" he said. "Let me guess who the rest of you are. You redheads must be O'Malleys, and there's no mistaking Jay's mother—the resemblance is startling."

He glanced inquiringly at Mr. Todd, who came forward to introduce himself. "Happy to meet you," Homer Kourides said. "Happy to meet all my new neighbors."

The silence in the room was so abrupt that it startled Jeremiah like a sonic boom. The people of Pineapple Place stood frozen where they were. Only their eyes moved as they looked at one another apprehensively. The seconds that went by seemed like hours.

Jeremiah felt so uneasy that he broke the silence with a nervous laugh. "We're not going to be neighbors anymore. We're moving to the North Pole."

"You're moving to Athens, Greece, and we're going with you," Homer Kourides announced.

Without being asked, he pulled a footstool close to Mr. Sweeny's armchair and sat down. "Ruby and I should never have moved to this town in the first place," he said. "I understand the same goes for you folks. You were aiming for Greece and missed, right? Well, Greece is where we want to be. We've got family there that will be glad to take us in until Ruby and I find a place to live—together."

Mr. Sweeny raised an eyebrow. "So what?"

"So when you move, you'll have two extra passengers. It ought to be a breeze for an old hand like you."

"It would be a breeze if I were inclined to do it," Mr. Sweeny said. "Unfortunately, I am not. Please go away."

Homer Kourides smiled apologetically. "I know it's in bad taste to insist, but I wish you'd change your mind. Unless you do, I'll be obliged to make you visible, every last one of you. My concoction has already infiltrated your drinking water."

The volcano exploded: Mr. Sweeny recovered his strength and leapt out of his chair. His wife rushed forward to steady him, but he pushed her away.

"Out of here!" he shouted. "Scram! Away! Push off! Stand not on the order of your going, but go at once! We're moving today, and until we go we'll keep our mouths shut tight. Not one drop of your infernal concoction will pass through our lips."

Jeremiah lost all hope, but Mrs. Pettylittle left his mother's side and moved to the center of the room.

"No," she said. "That's not the way it's going to be. Homer can't force you to swallow his concoction, but you can't force me to leave him, either. We're engaged to be married.''

There was a long, shocked silence that ended when Jeremiah broke into a cheer. ''Hooo-ray! That's wonderful!''

''It's not wonderful, it's a disaster,'' Mr. Sweeny said in a voice tense with rage. ''All the same, I don't see how it affects my decision.''

Mrs. Pettylittle slipped her arm through Homer Kourides' elbow. ''It needn't affect it at all,'' she said. ''If you refuse to bring Homer to Athens, Greece, we'll just stay here. Once we're married, I'm sure Ruby will be allowed to live with us, and you can go your merry way. Of course you may have a few problems rag-bagging, but with your superior brainpower, I'm sure you'll resolve them.''

The Sixth Day

23

On the morning after his street moved to Athens, Jeremiah Jenkins climbed the cedar tree. He climbed slowly, guiding Ruby's feet as she worked her way from branch to branch above him.

"What do you see?" he asked when she was near the top.

"Streets," Ruby panted. "City streets, and whitish houses that look foreign, and a lot of red-tile roofs. Off in the distance there are some skyscrapers, but here it's more old-fashioned."

Jeremiah pulled himself up to a higher branch. "How about the Acropolis, and the Parthenon?"

"I don't know. There's something up the hill that looks pretty much like the photo in Uncle Homer's book."

"And the Aegean Sea?"

A chorus of voices rose from the street below. "Jeremiah! Jeremiah! Where are you?"

Jeremiah peered through the branches and saw April and the O'Malley children.

"Jeremiah!" they called again.

"Why don't you answer them?" Ruby asked.

"Because this place is secret," he explained. "Except for you."

Ruby laughed. "Why do you need a secret place? You're already a secret person all your own. So is everybody else here. That's what's so nice about you: each one of you is different, but you get along together all the same. I don't think you should try to change."

A big grin spread over Jeremiah's face. "Too late— I've already changed!" he said.

Thrusting his head through the branches, he leaned out and shouted: "My name is Jay, not Jeremiah! Jay Jenkins! I'm Jay Jenkins of Pineapple Place!"

America's Favorite Stories
from Best-selling Author
BEVERLY CLEARY

HENRY AND BEEZUS
70914-7/$3.50 US/$4.25 Can

HENRY AND RIBSY
70917-1/$3.50 US/$4.25 Can

HENRY AND THE CLUBHOUSE
70915-1/$3.50 US/$4.25 Can

HENRY HUGGINS
70912-0/$3.50 US/$4.25 Can

BEEZUS AND RAMONA
70918-X/$3.50 US/$4.25 Can

RAMONA AND HER FATHER
70916-3/$3.50 US/$4.25 Can

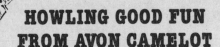

HOWLING GOOD FUN
FROM AVON CAMELOT

HOW TO BE A VAMPIRE IN ONE EASY LESSON
75906-3/$2.75 US/$3.25 CAN

ISLAND OF THE WEIRD
75907-1/$2.75 US/$3.25 CAN

THE MONSTER IN CREEPS HEAD BAY
75905-5/$2.75 US/$3.25 CAN

THINGS THAT GO BARK IN THE PARK
75786-9/$2.75 US/$3.25 CAN

YUCKERS! 75787-7/$2.75 US/$3.25 CAN

M IS FOR MONSTER 75423-1/$2.75 US/$3.25 CAN

BORN TO HOWL 75425-8/$2.50 US/$3.25 CAN

THERE'S A BATWING IN MY LUNCHBOX
75426-6/$2.75 US/$3.25 CAN

THE PET OF FRANKENSTEIN
75185-2/$2.50 US/$2.50 US/$3.25 CAN

Z IS FOR ZOMBIE 75686-2/$2.75 US/$3.25 CAN

MONSTER MASHERS
75785-0/$2.75 US/$3.25 CAN

MONSTERS 7/90